"If John D. M[...] kicked his meds, he'[...] Hopkins' The Licking Valley Coon Hunters Club.

"This one's a fictive breeder's field day. Forget Luther Burbank. Imagine Joe R. Lansdale's city cuz crossbred with one of Andrew Vacchs' surlier rural relatives, but with a whole lot of genetic material from the real author, Brian Hopkins. Now there's an experiment in literary biotechnology. Oh, yeah, and the vampires are just lagniappe! This is an in-you-face tale of today's weird science, bad behavior, and human cussedness that kicks butt.

"Hopkins' P.I., Martin Zolotow, is a cranky and tenacious guy who tries hard not to be likable, but you gotta admit he always gets his man -- or, more frequently, his woman. To read about him is to wince, and then eventually to grin. Plenty."

-- **Ed Bryant**

"There's something about Oklahoma, and it's not the wind whistling down the plain, though the wind -- and the rain -- does have a significant role to play in THE LICKING VALLEY COON HUNTERS CLUB as Brian Hopkins, who, perhaps, knows more about the state than he'd really like, paints a vivid panorama of violence, depravity and just a hint of things that just ain't the way they're supposed to be. You've heard of the fire and your've heard of the frying pan, now fasten your seat-belts and join Martin Zolotow, memory-impaired PI, for a visit to the Panhandle.

-- **Lynn Abbey**

"Coon Hunters -- the newest edition to the adventures of Martin Zolotow -- delivers Brian Hopkins at his finest. Wisecracking and eloquent, poetic and ready to kick ass at a moment's notice, Zolotow and his cross-wired brain are the perfect answer to a craving for suspense and mystery. Hopkins is one of the true new talents."

-- **David Niall Wilson**

"Imagine a parallel universe wherein Davis Grubb and Andrew Vaches had written a chase film for Sam Peckinpah, and you may have some idea of the surprising scope and depth of this short but damned impressive novel; suspenseful, violent, lean, poetic, and even thoughtful, THE LICKING VALLEY COON HUNTERS CLUB is a return to what originally made the thriller great, before brutality and shock were mistaken for action and suspense.

"Don't'be fooled by the length of this novel; Brian Hopkins packs more action, humor, and feeling into his streamlined narrative than any half-dozen of the so-called "suspense novels" on the shelves today. And what a refreshing change to find a central character who can easily take his place alongside Philip Marlowe or John Rambo -- simply because he's a little of both, with a touch of Jung thrown in for good measure."

-- **Gary A. Braunbeck**, *author of THINGS LEFT BEHIND and THE INDIFFERENCE OF HEAVEN*

"This is a very entertaining book. It has everything a P.I. book should... a hard-boiled but chivalrous P.I., lovely ladies in distress, quirky villains who repeatedly beat the hero to a pulp, and a plot that cracks along at the speed of a bullet. PLUS vampires and a science-fiction twist. Who could ask for anything more?

-- **Lee Killough**, *author of BLOOD WALK and BLOOD GAMES (Coming in spring 2001)*

The 2001 Bram Stoker Award
Winner for
"Best First Novel"

The Licking Valley Coon Hunters Club

(A Martin Zolotow Mystery)

by
Brian A. Hopkins

This is a work of fiction. All the characters and events portrayed in this book are fictitious, and any resemblance to real people is purely coincidental.

Note: Words and music to "You Never Even Called Me By My Name" copyright — 1975 by CBS, Inc. Written by Steve Goodman. Performed by David Allan Coe. Words and music to "Up Against the Wall Red Neck" copyright — 1973 by MCA Records, Inc. Written by Ray Wiley Hubbard. Performed by Jerry Jeff Walker.

ISBN 1-893687-25-2

First Edition Copyright © 2000 by Brian A. Hopkins
Second Edition Copyright © 2002 by Brian A. Hopkins

All rights reserved, including the right to reproduce this book or portions thereof in any form except for purposes of review.

Yard Dog Press
710 W. Redbud Lane
Alma, AR 72921-7247

http://www.yarddogpress.com

Edited by Selina Rosen
Technical Editor Lynn Stranathan
Cover art by Brand Whitlock

Printed in the United States of America
0 9 8 7 6 5 4 3 2 1

*For Debora —
A fun romp through
the wilds of Oklahoma.
Thanks!*

For the real "Coon Hunters," those supportive fans and friends who allow me to clog their mail boxes once or twice a month with my hopes and dreams.

ONE: *White Knights and Ladies — Oklahoma City and Igloos — Dirt Roads and Cadillacs — Vampires and Photographs — Rednecks and Baseball Bats*

Debbie turned back at the last minute. The flight attendant's outstretched hand hovered, just inches short of taking her boarding pass. The line of travelers crowded behind her frowned in unison. Debbie looked at Martin Zolotow with those incredible, brown, doe eyes, tears building in the corner of each, and said, "You know, Marty, I could stay. There's really no reason for going back."

He pulled her to the side so the other passengers could board the TWA flight, his big hands firm on the soft, bare flesh of her upper arms. It did not escape his attention that this was probably the last time he would touch her. He couldn't help but catalog the way the California sun played off her long, blonde hair and the unblemished copper of her thighs, knowing it was his last chance to do so. He tried to focus on her cute little upturned nose or her delicate ears, without letting the fact that he would never see them again bring him to his knees. His heart was a tremendous dead weight in the center of his chest. Numb. He refused to let it drag him down. He refused to let it dictate his actions.

"We've been over this, Deb." He tipped her chin up. "You go home and straighten things out with your folks. You take a job waiting tables or selling popcorn at the local theater. It doesn't have to be anything serious at first. You get your life straightened out…"

"Marty."

"...maybe you go to a local junior college; take some accounting courses and go to work at a bank. Maybe you meet a nice boy you used to know in school. Not a jock who used to feel you up between classes, but someone you never even noticed before. The president of the math club maybe. Some nerd who's just now blossoming into the kind of man most women don't realize they want until it's too late. Someone making good money designing computer chips for Texas Instruments."

"Marty."

"...you make a couple beautiful babies and you live to be an old, very happy grandmother."

She placed two fingers over his lips. "Marty, what I want to do is stay with you. I love you."

He kissed her fingers, pulled them away from his lips, and held her hand against his chest. "Deb, I'm more than twice your age. And the life I live…"

"Is not the kind to give a woman peace of mind," she interjected. "I've heard the song, Marty. What's really going on here is you refuse to let anyone get close to you. You refuse to let yourself love someone back." The first tear spilled from her right eye and painted a glistening trail down her cheek. "Damn it. I told myself I wasn't going to do this." She wiped fiercely at her eyes.

Zolotow swallowed and tried to find his voice.

"Every time you pull some hooker off the street and help her put her life back together, she falls in love with you. Don't you see that? And every time they start to get close, you send them packing. What is it, Marty? Are you afraid to love someone? Afraid something will happen to them if you do?"

"You're going to miss your flight," he croaked.

"I want to miss the goddamned flight!"

"Your parents will be waiting," he said. "I did a lot of talking to arrange this."

She choked back a sob. "You did a lot of talking to cover the real reason you're sending me away." She poked a finger at his chest. "You took me off the streets and made me *your* whore, Martin Zolotow! And now that you're tired of me, you're sending me home so you can feel you've done your community service work for the month." She was crying now. "Who'll it be next month, Marty? Who you gonna rescue next?"

"Debbie…"

"Go to hell," she snapped. She turned and cut into the line, thrusting her ticket at the flight attendant.

Glaring at Zolotow, the flight attendant tore away the stub and passed the ticket back to Debbie with a consoling, "You go on and board now, hon."

Debbie stomped down the ramp, turning at the last minute to yell, "You're nobody's fucking white knight, Martin Zolotow!"

Then she was gone, and he was left standing at the window in LAX with thirty or forty people glaring at him, hands in his pockets, a lump in his throat that he knew wouldn't go away no matter how much scotch he sent down after it. Despite the glares and an old woman who shook an umbrella at him and called him an asshole, he stood there until the plane backed out and taxied down the runway, bound for Dallas.

He whispered the second verse from Rossetti's "Remember," so softly that none could hear it, not even he:

> *"Yet if you should forget me for a while*
> *And afterwards remember, do not grieve:*
> *For if the darkness and corruption leave*
> *A vestige of the thoughts that once I had,*
> *Better by far you should forget and smile*
> *Than that you should remember and be sad."*

"Women," snickered someone behind him, "can't live with 'em, can't kill 'em." A hand fell on Zolotow's shoulder.

Zolotow looked back to find an emaciated specimen with purple splotched cheeks and red-rimmed eyes, thin greasy hair and coke-bottle glasses. The man's nails were long and sepia-tinted. "You might want to take that hand off me," Zolotow said softly.

"You might want to look down at my other hand," the

man said, smiling. His teeth were as yellow as old pine and at least two of them appeared to have been filed. There were no demarcations between each tooth, just heavy accumulation of brown plaque. His face was skeletal, the bloodshot eyes behind the thick glasses sunk deep in the center of dark craters. His skin was as pale as his scalp-cut hair was dark. His collarbones stood out like railroad ties. There was a crucifix dangling from his left ear lobe. His accent was Midwestern redneck.

In the man's right hand, pressed now against Zolotow's side, was a hypodermic syringe, the cap removed to expose the slender needle. The plunger of the syringe was firmly planted in the man's palm. One push and ...

"Is that blood?" Zolotow asked.

"Yep. Mine."

"What do you want?"

The man removed his hand from Zolotow's shoulder and pulled two plane tickets from his shirt pocket. "Seeing as how we're at the airport and all, I thought we'd take us a trip. Friend of mine wants to meet you, Zolotow."

"And if I don't want to go?"

The man's grin widened until his face was little more than dirty teeth and bad breath stretched ear to ear. The broken vessels in his cheeks looked like they were going to bleed. "I got maybe three months to live, Zolotow." He nudged Zolotow in the ribs with the syringe, one crooked finger preventing the needle from sinking through Zolotow's shirt and into flesh. "You want to make that trip with me? I reckon there's easier ways to die."

Zolotow tried to smile back. "Business has been slow anyway. I guess I could use a vacation."

"Oh, this ain't no vacation. And business done picked up for you. Play your cards right, and you'll come out of this smelling like a rose."

"A rose?"

"How 'bout like a really nice, underage whore? That comparison more to your liking?" The skeleton chuckled softly. "Now walk with me. We got a flight to catch. Try anything stupid, and I'll put this needle in you."

"Where are we going?" Martin asked, thinking he should have brought his notepad. He hated waking up somewhere and not knowing where he was.

"Just three gates down."

"No. I mean *where*."

"Oh!" Realization dawned on the dying man's face like sudden indigestion. "Oklahoma City, Zolotow. The heartland of America."

Watching from the window seat, Zolotow was completely unimpressed with Oklahoma City's skyline. Downtown appeared as if it might occupy, at most, two or three blocks in L.A. He'd been through here once before, years ago, in pursuit of a felon he preferred not to think about now, but he'd seen very little of the town. It didn't look as if he'd missed much. It certainly didn't look like a second visit was warranted.

It had been a long, boring flight. Death, which is what Zolotow had decided to call his abductor, had raised the arm rest between them and sat through the whole flight with the hypodermic needle against Zolotow's side. When Zolotow had asked to go to the restroom, Death had showed him those rotten teeth and said, "Suck it up, Zolotow. You ain't going nowhere till we land in OKC." Zolotow had tried to start a conversation with one of the flight attendants, but Death had politely told her that his friend by the window was a known rapist, child molester, arsonist, and militia goon, and that Death, a federal agent, was taking him to OKC for questioning on the Murrah bombing. "It's taken us several years," he said, "but we think we might have located John Doe Number Two." He winked at her. Zolotow knew that federal agents transporting suspects are, of course, required to be declared to flight crews before boarding. The flight attendant knew Death wasn't telling the truth. She seemed to take it as a really bad joke, and from that point on wouldn't even look their way. Death had said very little to Zolotow after that, refusing to answer even the most innocent of questions. Zolotow was tired and hungry and he still had to go to the bathroom. By the time they landed, he was ready to kill someone.

Zolotow expected them to go directly to curbside where a dark van would speed by, pausing long enough for him to be shoved inside. That's what always happened in the movies. It turned out that they had luggage. He stood at the carousel with Death for fifteen minutes, crossing and uncrossing his legs, looking like a five year old or a pregnant woman with a bladder problem.

"It's going to be real embarrassing for you when I piss my pants," he told Death.

"Not to mention how embarrassing it'll be for your ownself," Death replied. Then he pointed. "There. Grab that."

It was an Igloo cooler, one of the really big red ones designed so an Okie can go all weekend without having to send the wife out for more beer. It was dripping condensation and cold to the touch. Someone had wrapped about five rolls of duct tape all around it. It was going to take a major archeological expedition to get it open. Zolotow heaved it up on his shoulder, expecting to hear half-melted ice sloshing around inside, but there was only a little shifting from within. Whatever was inside was being kept cold with something other than ice. Maybe it was T-bones and baby-back ribs loaded with those plastic freezer packs.

"We going to a barbecue?" Zolotow asked.

"Shut up. Out those doors over there."

There was a blue Ford Bronco waiting at the curb and two gentlemen dressed in business suits and cowboy hats. "Nice boots," Zolotow told one of them. "Rodeo in town this week?"

"Shut up," the man responded. He was carrying a folded newspaper. He opened it just enough for Zolotow to see the nickel-plated S&W nine millimeter semi-auto inside. "Cooler goes in the back," and he popped the hatch on the Bronco. He had mean blue eyes, two criss-crossing scars on his right cheek, and tobacco-stained teeth.

Zolotow heaved the cooler off his shoulder and into the back of the Ford.

"Get in the truck," Death snapped. He lead the way around the side of the vehicle while one of the guys in the suits kept Zolotow covered with the loaded newspaper and the second one closed the back of the Bronco. There was a trash can on the curb. Death tossed the hypodermic inside.

"That's a bio-hazard, you know," Zolotow told him. "Some poor sanitation worker could get hurt on that thing."

Death grinned. "You think I give a rat's ass? Now get in the fucking truck 'fore I have Earl there kick your nuts up into the back of your throat."

"Earl would do that?"

Earl grunted and something cold flashed in the depths of his blue eyes. "Fuckin' A, I would." The scars on his cheek rearranged themselves as he smiled.

Zolotow got in the back seat and slid all the way across. First thing he noticed was that there wasn't a handle on the inside of the door. Second thing he noticed was the chains in the floorboard. There were two sets. Ankle cuffs at one end. Bolted to the floorboard at the other.

Death started to get in the front seat, but the guy getting in on the driver's side waved him off. "Ain't no fucking way you're sitting next to me, you sick sonofabitch. You get in the back with Magnum P.I. there."

"Fuck you," Death replied, but Earl prodded him with his newspaper.

"Do what Billy Ray said."

Death crawled in the back next to Zolotow, spitting and cussing all the while. Billy Ray got in and started the truck. Earl got in the passenger side. As they pulled away, Earl let the newspaper drop to the floorboard and reached back through the seats to place the muzzle of the nine millimeter against Zolotow's right knee cap.

"First time you fuck up, Mr. Private Eye, you'll be hobbling through the rest of this here big adventure you're about to have. Understand?"

Zolotow tried to smile as big as he'd seen Death do in L.A. Mimicking their drawl, he said, "Ya'll don't mind me. I'll just be sitting here praying for a chance to pee."

Billy Ray looked up in the rearview mirror. "You ain't let this man take a piss, Coop? All the way from L.A., you ain't let the poor bastard go to the bathroom?"

"How the hell was I supposed to let him take a piss?" Death fired back.

"Ain't right, not letting the man take care of his bodily functions," Earl said.

"Well, he'll just have to hold it now," said Billy Ray.

"I was afraid you were going to say that," said Zolotow.

"Shut up," all three of them barked.

Leaving the airport, Zolotow discovered giant, forty-foot tall arrows protruding from the ground by the side of the road. Several were leaning precariously, and he wondered if they'd been set that way or if a tornado had come through. Oklahoma, he thought he remembered, was big on tornadoes. The only remotely interesting sight, besides the arrows, was several oil wells pumping away in the surrounding fields. He wondered if they were real or just for the tourists. Oklahoma was big on tourism, too, wasn't it?

His sarcasm failed to keep him entertained for long, but none of the rednecks wanted to talk. There was little out the Bronco's windows to occupy his mind, downtown lying in the opposite direction, and he wondered just exactly what Okies did with their spare time. Nothing too exciting, as none of them appeared to be in any hurry to get where they were going. The slow-moving interstate traffic was the first big difference between California and Oklahoma that he noticed. Three out of every four vehicles they passed were pickup trucks, spare tires, lawn chairs, and scrap lumber stacked in their beds. The pickup image seemed somehow appropriate, in keeping with their speed, as if all of Oklahoma were running at a slower pace than he was used to. His second observation was the clear blue sky. The air was clean and sharp. No smog. The legendary and much-maligned Oklahoma wind was obviously on vacation. He could see where the wind might be a pain in the ass, though, as there was already dust everywhere. He vaguely recalled an old joke. Why does the wind always blow in Oklahoma? Cause Texas sucks. Heat waves dominated the pavement. The sun tried to melt through the window pane and cook his arm. He was reminded that this was where the flatlands of Kansas and the semi-desert of Texas met. He was a long way from paradise.

They took Interstate 40 westbound out of town. Watching twisted blackjack oaks and other stunted Midwestern trees slip past the window, Zolotow tried to think about something other than a nice rest area with complete facilities. Billy Ray kept his eyes on the road, sticking to the speed limit. Earl kept the S&W pressed against Zolotow's knee, a look of utter boredom on his face or maybe it was just a complete lack of intelligence. Zolotow wasn't sure. Coop ... a.k.a. Death ... leaned against the door and looked as if he was going to throw up. Zolotow realized the stress of the kidnapping must have been pretty taxing for a man in Coop's medical condition. He tried to work up some compassion for the man, but failed.

Just past someplace called El Reno, Oklahoma, Billy Ray took an exit and turned south. A couple miles later, the blacktop started giving out. Before it vanished completely, they turned off on a rutted, red dirt road. The Bronco bounced this way and that, torturing Zolotow's bladder.

In short order, the dirt road became something that might have aspirations for one day being a full-fledged trail. It wound through cedars and oaks, down red clay gullies and over weather-beaten hummocks. Clumps of Indian sage grass whispered against the bottom of the Bronco. Tree branches scratched at the doors. The antennae went *spang!* at one point and Zolotow pointed out that such treatment would surely screw up their radio reception. The three rednecks told him to shut up again. Several miles crept by without the scenery changing. The Bronco's air conditioning began to labor.

And then they dropped down a steep bank and came abruptly upon a farm pond. There were a couple cows loitering about, ankle deep in red mud, working their jaws as if they hadn't a care in the world. There was a silver Cadillac parked by the pond, its windows tinted so dark that it was impossible to see inside. There was a pickup truck, pale yellow and empty, looking as if it had sat there collecting dust for weeks. Billy Ray shut off the engine. Earl took the gun away from Zolotow's knee. "Go ahead."

"There?" Zolotow asked, pointing at the Caddy.

"Yeah."

"You want me to get out and go over to the car there?"

Earl pointed the gun. "Go."

"Well, I would, but..."

Billy Ray turned around in the seat. "Quit fucking around!"

Zolotow held up his hands. "I'm not trying to be difficult here, it's just that someone at Ford screwed you over good."

"What?"

Zolotow pointed a thumb at the door. "There's no handle on the inside of this door. I think you ought to maybe stop by your Ford dealer and..."

"Shit." Billy Ray jumped out the driver's side door and reached for the outside handle of Zolotow's door.

Zolotow was suddenly in motion. As Billy Ray exited the vehicle, Zolotow slapped Earl's pistol aside and lunged over the front seats, driving Earl's head into the dashboard. Hanging half over the seats, he kicked Coop several times in the head while pounding Earl senseless with his elbow. By the time Billy Ray got the back door open and leaned inside with his own gun drawn, Zolotow had Earl's nine millimeter. For a moment, the impasse held, both men with their guns trained on the other. Coop and Earl were huddled in their seats, cursing and holding their heads. Earl's nose was bleeding. Coop had the red imprint from the bottom of one of Zolotow's loafers on his forehead.

The front doors of the Cadillac opened and two black men with Uzis stepped out, the machine guns leveled at the Bronco. The back window of the Cadillac rolled down and a fat, black man the size of a Sherman tank leaned out and said, "Zolotow? Martin Zolotow?"

"This is him, boss," said Billy Ray.

"Please put down that gun and join me, Mr. Zolotow."

Zolotow blinked as sweat ran from his forehead into his eye. Now that the Bronco was standing wide open, the Oklahoma summer was stifling. "If you don't mind, I think I'd rather you just called me a cab back to the airport. I'm tired of these goons telling me to shut up."

"Cabs are hard to get out here in the sticks," replied the black man. "Come hear what I have to say, and if you aren't interested I'll see you back to the airport myself."

"I already know I'm not interested."

"Don't be so sure. I'm prepared to offer you a lot of money for something well within your capabilities as a private detective."

Zolotow cleared his throat. "My job interviews generally go a lot smoother than this."

"And I apologize for that. The boys do get carried away sometimes."

"You saying you didn't send them to kidnap me?" Zolotow asked. "You saying they took the initiative based on something you said? Like maybe you were sitting on the porch with Auntie Em, sipping lemonade and scanning the horizon for tornadoes, when you said, 'Gee, it'd be nice to meet old Marty Zolotow sometime.' And your redneck cousins here, Billy Ray Joe Bob and Earl I-carry-a-newspaper-but-I-can't-read-it, got together with their AIDS-infested buddy and came to get me?"

"Auntie Em's in Kansas," mumbled Billy Ray, his aim unwavering.

And, "I can too read," grumbled Earl.

And, "I ain't got AIDS," hissed Coop.

The fat man pulled out a handkerchief and wiped his brow. "It's damn hot out here, Mr. Zolotow. I'm gonna roll up my window now and quit wasting all this nice air conditioning. You think about whether you want to come hear what I have to say or whether you want me to tell Ernie and Bubba there to open up with their Uzis."

Zolotow wondered how much longer before he started forgetting all the rednecks' names. He needed to take notes. He needed to write down what clues he'd gathered before the case became too complicated to follow. The Igloo, that bore some note taking. The Igloo damn sure smelled like a clue. But his notepad was sitting on his desk in San Valencez ... where he was supposed to be.

He looked over his shoulder at the two men who had emerged from the front of the Caddy. Ernie and Bubba looked like serious brothers. They looked like they'd open up if Fat Boy told them to. They looked like they could care less if the Uzi spray also took out I-can-read Earl and I'm-sick-but-I-ain't-got-AIDS Coop.

Billy Ray smiled and slipped his sidearm back under his jacket. Backing out of the open door, he whispered, "See ya, hotshot." He moved to a spot about ten feet behind the Bronco. Out of the line of fire.

Earl crouched down on the floorboard. Coop disappeared behind the seats.

Zolotow let out a heavy sigh. When he looked back again, the rear window on the Caddy had rolled up, revealing nothing but a mirrored reflection of himself, looking stupid all hunched over in the front of the Bronco. "Shit," Zolotow mumbled. He lowered the hammer on the S&W and backed out of the driver's side door. The Uzis tracked his movement. Feet firmly planted in the red mud, he slipped the S&W into his waistband, stood up, and turned around. He smiled at Ernie and Bubba and held up a finger. "Just a sec, boys. Tell the boss I'll be right with him." Then he walked out in front of the Bronco, down to the side of the pond and over to an appropriate tree.

The rear window of the Caddy slid down with a hiss. "What the hell's he doing?" the fat, black man asked.

Ernie or Bubba. Zolotow wasn't sure which was which, called back: "Looks like he's taking a piss."

"Taking a piss? Well, when he's done, take that pistol away from him and bring him here."

The man in the back of the Cadillac was *bigger* than a Sherman tank. He took up at least three fourths of the back seat. He was wearing an expensive suit that had to have been custom-tailored — Zolotow knew for a fact that this sort of suit wasn't available in your average big and tall shop — and the typical Oklahoma footwear, cowboy boots. He smelled of expensive cologne and ... something else. It took Zolotow a few minutes to figure it out. The guy smelled like Reese's Peanut Butter Cups.

As the door closed behind Zolotow, the fat man tossed a folder at the detective.

"I think you've mistaken me for someone else," Zolotow said.

"You're Martin Zolotow," said the fat man. His speech was precise, educated. While he talked, his nostrils flared constantly, as if it was a struggle to talk and draw breath at the same time, as if it took a supreme effort to supply oxygen to that much bulk. "You started out walking a beat in some little burg south of L.A. You were a police detective for fifteen years when a partner of yours was torn apart by ... What'd you call her? A *were-leopard*?" From the front seat, Ernie and Bubba sniggered. "After some serious psychiatric evaluation and a leave of absence, you turned up in San Antonio in the middle of a serial murder case. You'd been shot several times and there were some dead bodies to account for, one of them a San Antonio detective."

"I was cut pretty bad, too," Zolotow added. Rolling up his sleeve, he showed Ernie and Bubba the eight inch scar on his forearm.

"Shit. That ain't nothing," one of them said and started to unbutton his shirt.

"Ernie!" snapped the fat man.

"Sorry, boss."

Zolotow made a mental note. Ernie was the one with the feather hat band.

"Despite all this mayhem, San Antonio P.D. vindicated you. They even gave you credit for solving the case and saving the life of another San Antonio detective. You went back to California and they offered you an early retirement "

Zolotow snorted. "That's one way of putting it."

"You opened your own private investigation service and in the last five years have somehow managed to attract every nut case client in L.A. Funny thing is, even L.A.P.D. uses your services, calling you any time they have something unusual. You've a reputation for solving the most bizarre of cases. You're something of an expert at interfacing with the most seedy underground environments. You've been featured in the *L.A. Times* at least three times that I know of. Your picture was on the cover of *Criminal Law*. And last year, there was even an L.A. underground movement to name a women's shelter after you."

"You left out the three articles in *The National Enquirer*," Zolotow chuckled. He lifted the folder. "Is all that in this little folder? You know there was a really good picture of me with that one article — what was it called? Oh, yeah: 'Ghostbusting Detective Takes a Bite Out of Werewolf Cult.' I loved that one."

"According to your psych evaluations, you've got serious problems with women, alcohol, memory, and authority figures."

"You left out my weakness for rocky road." Zolotow slapped his stomach. "I eat way too much ice cream."

The fat man smiled indulgently. "We've done our homework, Mr. Zolotow. Or may I call you Zolo?"

"Mr. Zolotow will do just fine. For the moment, you have me at a distinct disadvantage. I've met Coop and Billy Ray and Earl." The three of them were, at that moment, leaning against the blue Bronco, waiting. "In the front seat are my good friends Ernie and Bubba, the Uzi brothers." Damn, he'd already forgotten which was which. It had something to do with the hats. "But I don't know who the hell you are."

The fat man extended a coal black lump of a hand on which the five fingers were merely sausage-shaped stubs. For a minute, Zolotow thought the man had been the victim of some bizarre table saw accident, but then he saw that all the knuckle joints were indeed still there. The fingers were just buried, like everything else on the man, in fat. The hand looked like a black cow's udder.

"Tobias Weatherford Washington, Mr. Zolotow. My friends call me Toby."

Zolotow shook his hand, found it clammy and cold. Despite the fat, Tobias Weatherford Washington had a crushing grip, which he demonstrated without even a smile. Zolotow swallowed a grimace, determined he'd hear bones crack before he yelped, but the fat man eased off after a moment, allowing Zolotow to wipe his throbbing hand on his pants leg.

"You want to tell me why you've kidnapped me?"

"Kidnapped is an inappropriate description, Mr. Zolotow. We're not asking anyone for ransom money."

"That's good," Zolotow said. "I don't think you'd find anyone willing to pay you much. I'm sure I'd be a lot more trouble than I'm worth. What with plane tickets and all, I'm sure you're already out more than…"

"Shut up, Mr. Zolotow."

Zolotow frowned. "I'm getting damn tired of you Okies telling me to shut up."

"I'm prepared to offer you a hundred thousand dollars to find my daughter and return her safely to me."

"Come again?"

"A hundred thousand dollars."

"What's the catch? Why don't you just have the redneck posse here round her up?"

"What do you know about vampires, Mr. Zolotow?"

"What?"

"Vampires."

"Bloodsucking, don't come out in the daylight vampires, or are we talking about your average lawyer?"

"You see Mr. Cooper there?" Washington asked. "He thinks he's a vampire."

Zolotow laughed. "Why ain't he melting in the sunlight then? And what's with the crucifix earring?"

"I didn't say he *was* a vampire, Mr. Zolotow. I said he thought he was one."

"Is that how he got so sickly looking? He suck the neck of some guy with HIV?"

"He's sick because he's been denying himself human blood."

"Kicking the habit?"

"Yes."

"They don't sell a patch for that? Some gum maybe?"

Washington ignored the jibe, but both Ernie and Bubba had to hide grins. "Until recently, Mr. Cooper was in the employ of my competitor and occasional associate, a gentleman by the name of Jimmy McDevitt."

Zolotow thought that might explain why Earl and Billy Ray didn't seem overly fond of Cooper — ignoring, of course, the obvious reasons for wanting nothing to do with him. Zolotow was fast reaching overload, though. "You don't have a paper and a pen, do you? I really need to write some of this down."

"Just pay attention, Mr. Zolotow. Jimmy McDevitt has a club in Beaver, Oklahoma. It's a ... vampire club."

"Do they call it that? A vampire club, I mean. Can you look them up in the yellow pages under V?"

"The club is called the Licking Valley Coon Hunters," Washington said. His voice was growing softer and it was obvious that he was running out of patience. He'd quit showing Zolotow his large white teeth. "They have my daughter and they will kill her. I want you to infiltrate their organization and bring her back to me. I will pay you a hundred thousand dollars."

Zolotow scratched his head. "You didn't answer my question. Why don't you just go in there yourself? You appear to have the muscle, the firepower. You know that they have her."

"McDevitt knows my men. He would recognize them. Though I know he has her, I don't know where he's keeping her. For the moment, he doesn't know she's my daughter and that might be all that's keeping her alive. If one of my boys went in, McDevitt would know something was up. I need an unknown to join their ranks and bring her out. Cooper's the key to getting in."

"One of their own?"

"Right."

"And you trust the bloodsucker?"

"No. But he's all I've got. And he did bring me word that my daughter was there."

"I don't quite understand how she wound up there," Zolotow said.

"That's unimportant. I just need you to bring her back to me."

"You're not giving me much to work with."

"I know, but you'll have Cooper."

"Who might go into bloodsucking withdrawal at any moment."

"Your jokes are wearing thin."

"So is my patience. I'll take that ride to the airport now."

"It's a lot of money, Mr. Zolotow."

"I'm really not into that whole Hollywood wealth accumulation thing."

Washington reached into his jacket and pulled out an envelope. He slipped his fat fingers into the unsealed top and pulled out a Polaroid photo which he laid atop the folder on Zolotow's lap. The photo showed Zolotow and Debbie going through the metal detectors at LAX. "Beautiful young lady," remarked the fat man.

Zolotow said nothing.

Washington pulled out a second photo and laid it atop the first. The second photo showed Debbie walking through the gate to her plane, chin up, not looking back at Zolotow, who was standing, out of focus, to one side. "In some states, particularly in Oklahoma, she'd be considered too young for what I imagine you did to her, Zolo. I think in Oklahoma, you'd be charged with statutory rape."

"Fuck you."

Washington pulled out a third photo. "Good thing this little lady's home safe and sound." He laid the photo atop the others. It showed Debbie deplaning in what must be the Dallas-Fort Worth airport. An older couple were there to greet her. All three were crying. "'Home is the place where, when you have to go there, they have to take you in.' Wouldn't you agree, Zolo?"

"Robert Frost," Zolotow whispered. Their research must have been extensive if they knew of his penchant for poetry.

"But home isn't always as safe as we'd like it to be, is it? There are accidents in every home from time to time." He set out a fourth photo. A mini van, in a driveway before a small but well-kept home. Green grass. Neatly trimmed hedges. Rain gutters painted a bright white. There were three figures in the driveway. Zolotow didn't really have to look closely to know who they were. "There's a chink in every man's armor, Zolo."

"Only my friends call me that."

"We're going to be great friends," Washington said softly. "You, my knight in shining armor, will slay the vampires for me."

"This is blackmail," Zolotow said. "I think blackmailers are lodged right next to statutory rapists in most penitentiaries."

"That may be. But I don't think you'll complain to anyone." Washington laid a final photo atop all the others.

A hammock in the sunshine. Debbie's face in close-up against a pale blue pillow, soft tree branch shadows marking her cheeks. She must have been tired after the long flight and the excitement of being reunited with her parents. She and Zolotow hadn't slept much the night before. An afternoon nap in the back yard, in the hammock, beneath some oak trees, where she felt safe. Her eyes were closed. Her lips were slightly parted. Zolotow had often sat up at night and watched her sleeping ... just ... like ... that.

"I'll trade you, Zolo."

Zolotow picked up the top photo and slipped it into his shirt pocket, next to his heart, which had gone cold and still.

"I'll trade you the life of my daughter ... for the life of your whore."

Tires slipping in the mud, the Cadillac pulled away and left Zolotow standing there with Coop and Earl and Billy Ray. Tobias Weatherford Washington had taken everything but the photo in Zolotow's shirt pocket: the other Polaroids, the folder, the S&W, his wallet and his keys ... his bravado. Zolotow was barely breathing. His arms hung lifeless at his side. He was trying to think, but his mind was stuck in a loop that kept saying, "If I don't do what they want, they'll hurt Debbie." When he tried to think of a way out of the situation, all he could think about was how far it was to Dallas. He thought he could drive there in about three hours. A plane might get him there quicker if he was lucky enough to catch one leaving. Maybe he could rent a private jet.

"Earl and me will take the truck," Billy Ray told Coop. "We got some things to take care of. You take dipshit and head on out for Beaver."

Zolotow watched the Cadillac as it climbed over the hollow in which the pond lay. When it was out of sight, he turned, determined to put on whatever facade was necessary to convince the rednecks that he was prepared to follow through with Washington's plan. It was important that he stall for time until he could figure out what to do. "Just where the hell is Beaver, Oklahoma, anyway?" he asked.

While Zolotow's back had been turned, Earl had reached into one of the vehicles and retrieved a baseball bat. He swung it viciously at Zolotow's right knee.

Crack!

Zolotow went down in the mud, his knee exploding with pain.

"You're some kinda smartass, Mr. California Private Dick." Earl swung again and the bat landed solidly against Zolotow's side. Zolotow bit through his lip and tried to breathe. It felt as if his lungs had collapsed. He couldn't take in any air, which was just as well because he didn't want to scream in front of these bastards.

Billy Ray wrestled the bat from Earl's hands. "Don't kill the sonofabitch, Earl!"

Earl kicked Zolotow in the same ribs. It felt as if jagged ends of broken bone had just been driven out the other side. Another kick followed, this one glancing off the detective's shoulder. Another one in the ribs again. One in the ass. One to the same throbbing knee. Zolotow scrambled through the mud, trying to escape the blows but discovering that very little of his body was responding to his commands.

Coop bent down and grabbed Zolotow by the hair. He lifted Zolotow's face up out of the mud. For the first time, Zolotow noticed the color of his eyes. They were a pale blue-white — Siberian Husky eyes. "This is for saying I got AIDS." Coop drew back a fist and smashed it into Zolotow's nose. Zolotow was actually grateful. The punch made him suck air into his burning lungs. Blood, pumping from his nose, was sucked in with the air, though, and he began to choke.

"Shit! Not the face, Coop!" Billy Ray bellowed. "How

the hell you gonna take him to McDevitt if his face is all black and blue?"

"We'll think of something," Coop answered, drawing back his fist and hitting Zolotow several more times. He opened a cut over the detective's eye. Busted his lip. Just before Coop dropped his face back into the mud, Zolotow saw the would-be-vampire lick the blood from his knuckles.

Zolotow wasn't sure which confused him more, the sudden camaraderie of the three men or the fact that they expected him to perform his job after such a beating. He could only surmise that their common dislike for him had momentarily bonded them and that they really didn't give a shit whether he rescued Washington's daughter or not.

Earl kicked him a couple more times. Zolotow was beyond counting how many or noticing exactly where they struck.

"That's enough," said Billy Ray.

Earl and Coop backed off. Zolotow spit blood and mud and tried to speak. It took him a couple tries to get it out. "Thanks, Billy Ray. I owe you one. Maybe I'll kill your sorry ass last."

"Fuck you," Billy Ray said and hit him across the lower back with the baseball bat.

Zolotow blacked out. He came to a couple minutes later as he was being dumped across the back seat of the Bronco. He thought then that it was a good thing he'd gone to the bathroom earlier. Then he smelled something foul and realized he might not have escaped that embarrassment entirely. A second later, he realized he was smelling cow shit.

The Bronco's engine growled to life. "Yeehaw! Beaver, Oklahoma, here we come!" yelled Coop. The Bronco slewed sideways in the mud, spun around to climb the hill, and bounced so hard that Zolotow was thrown to the floor.

He lay there and tried not to move.

Interlude: "Is that prostitute still living with you?"

Zolotow glared at the police psychologist. She was too pretty to be in this line of work. The department should fire her and hire a wizened old priest. A priest would nod his balding head knowingly while hearing their confessions, recognizing temptation and sin even as he advised against them, his lips set in a unwavering, judgmental line instead of softly smiling in Dr. Mary Ellis' condescending way. Her smile said she understood their temptations, maybe even desired them. It was a vicarious, voyeuristic smile. She wanted nothing more than to hear the absolute worst that they'd done. Maybe she was just writing a book in her spare time, but Zolotow suspected she got off on the stories her clients brought her each week. A priest would occasionally react with shock, reprehension ... maybe even fear. Ellis would lean forward, the pink tip of her tongue gripped in her teeth, her long legs crossed as tight as mating snakes.

"Well?" *Go ahead*, her eyes said, *feed me every titillating detail*.

"Who I'm living with is hardly the department's concern."

"It is when it affects your job performance."

"There haven't been any complaints about my job performance."

"And I'm here to see that there aren't any. I'm also here to watch over the psychological well-being of the officers in this department, to watch for indicators that might fortell the emergence of a mental health problem. Preventive medicine, if you will."

And so they went, verbally fencing back and forth, getting nowhere. Zolotow watched the clock on the wall, hanging there next to her UCLA diploma. He was required to sit through one hour of this each week. As the minute hand slipped past its lower apex and started the long, slow climb back toward the hour, he tried to convince himself he could continue to put up with it. Putting himself in their shoes, he admitted that he'd given them more than enough reasons to require these sessions. Sometimes *he* wondered if he wasn't looney.

"In the last three years, you've lived with eight different women, Detective Zolotow."

Eight that you know of, he thought, but did not say. He stared at her legs and wondered what she was doing for dinner. Would a relationship with her help or hinder the psychological healing the department obviously thought he required?

"Six of those women were prostitutes."

"Ex-prostitutes," he said.

She referenced a folder from the stack on her desk. "Two of these women have subsequently been arrested for soliciting."

He shrugged. "Two out of six isn't bad, though. Even you'd have to admit that, Dr. Ellis. How many prostitutes hit the streets again after we arrest them? I'm guessing it's a lot higher percentage than two out of six. I'd say my reform program is significantly more effective than the State's."

"So you think you're running a community service? A prostitute reform program?"

"I said nothing of the sort," he answered carefully, precisely, aware that there was probably a tape recorder somewhere in her office. "In my years on the force, I've merely encountered a lot of people, some of them women, who needed a hand. Occasionally, I've been in a position to offer one."

She frowned at him. Tried to stare him down. How do you argue altruism? How do you tell a man he was wrong to help people when he could? Finally, she went back to her notes. "This woman living with you now ... Lizelle Blue." The way she said the name indicated she did not believe it could be found on any birth certificate. "It says here that she has AIDS."

Zolotow nodded. "That's correct."

Dr. Ellis closed the folder with a crisp slap. "Well, then, don't you think that presents a potential health hazard to yourself and to other members of this department?"

"No, I don't."

"How can you say that?" she asked incredulously. "Surely you see you're in danger of contracting the virus from this woman, Detective Zolotow! Even if you don't pass it on, there's always the risk that you could."

"You're assuming, Dr. Ellis, that I'm having sex with Lizelle." He looked her directly in the eyes. "I'm not."

Before she could control it, her eyes showed her shock. And something else: she looked disappointed, disappointed that the story wasn't as juicy as she'd hoped. And maybe one other thing: she looked intrigued. Interested. She'd suddenly discovered Martin Zolotow was a lot more complex than she'd first thought. Zolotow decided then and there that a relationship with her would do his career serious damage. Not that that would stop him if he was interested in her. He'd suddenly realized he wasn't interested in her at all.

"Then —" She hesitated, looking for the proper question. When she couldn't find it, she simply asked, "Why?"

"Because she needed my help, Dr. Ellis. Is that so hard to understand?"

TWO: *Greasy Burgers and Country Music — Cleaning Up and Taking Charge — Ambushed and Beaver Bound — Hog Farms and Hasty Lies — Dark Barns and Desperate Whispers*

He slept.

How long, he wasn't sure, but when he woke up the sun had gone down. The Bronco was stopped, engine idling, and there were blue neon lights coming in through the windows.

"Will there be anything else?" squawked a metallic voice.

"That's it," replied Coop from the front seat.

"Your total comes to nine eighty-three. Please pull around to the window."

"I hope you ordered some aspirin," Zolotow groaned around swollen lips.

"Shut up," Coop growled. "Don't get up off the floor or I'll give you another beating." The Bronco pulled forward.

"No problem." Zolotow couldn't have moved if he'd wanted to. His body was a cramped comma of agony wedged between the rear bench seat and the front bucket seats. The chains on the floorboard were digging into his hip and shoulder. He was too big a man to fit into such a small place. He was too big a man to hurt all over like this. Pain spread over this much surface area was worse than death. He tried to raise his head and discovered that he was stuck to the carpet with dried blood.

Coop exchanged money with someone at a drive through window. A paper sack dropped into the passenger seat. The smell of greasy hamburgers invaded the interior of the Bronco.

Zolotow thought about throwing up, but decided it would hurt too much.

The Bronco pulled away from the drive through, bounced over a speed bump that nearly caused Zolotow to scream, and then they were back out on the road, picking up speed.

"You can sit up now," Coop said. "I've got burgers and fries and cokes. Oh! Hot apple pies, too."

"Wonderful."

"What's that?"

"I can't move."

"Say again?"

Zolotow decided he was mumbling into the carpet that was plastered to his face. He tried again to lift his head, was rewarded with a ringing in his ears and a sixteen penny nail driven through the back of his skull. He persisted. The carpet peeled away with a sound like the separating halves of a Velcro strip.

"Somebody call an ambulance," Zolotow croaked.

"There's a picnic area I know of," Coop replied. "Down the road a piece. 'Bout fifteen minutes from here. We'll stop there, and you can clean up some. You smell like shit."

"Cow shit," Zolotow mumbled. Some of it was coming back to him. He clawed at the seat and tried to get up off the floor. There were a dozen knives in his ribs. He couldn't remember how they'd gotten there. When he got up on his knees, the right knee sank alligator teeth into every nerve ending in that side of his body.

"You okay back there?" Coop chuckled.

"Just dandy," Zolotow told him. "Something make you think otherwise?"

"Yeah. You screamed."

Zolotow rolled up onto the seat and lay there panting, staring at the roof of the Bronco. "Where are we?" he gasped.

"Just left Woodward."

"Woodward?"

"Yeah. Little podunk town in the middle of nowhere."

Obviously Zolotow had forgotten more than he thought. "Where are we going?"

"Beaver. Got about sixty, seventy miles to go. Hey, you like country music?" Coop reached down and switched on the radio. Country twang erupted from the Bronco's speakers and Coop sang along, his voice an octave or three too high:

*"Well I was drunk, the day my mama got outta prison,
And I went to pick her up in the rain,
But before I could get to the station in my pickup... truck,
She got runned over by a damned old train."*

"Why don't you just fucking shoot me and get it over with?" Zolotow asked. "I think this kind of torture violates the Geneva Convention."

"Shut your mouth! Country music is God's music. Ain't much use for a man what don't like country music." And he continued to sing, while Zolotow plugged his ears.

Zolotow tried to take stock of the situation. He was in a Bronco with some country western singer named Coop who had beaten the shit out of him. No, wait... there had been others: Earl and Billy Ray. Earl was fond of baseball bats.

They'd just driven through some place called Woodward. Woodward, California? He'd never heard of it. Maybe he wasn't in California? He shut his eyes and tried to think. He'd been taken against his will. Coop, the country western star? No. Coop, the vampire. (Vampire? Was that some bizarre nickname or what?) Earl with his bat. And Billy Ray. They wanted something from him. Something he knew? Something he'd hidden? They'd tried to beat something out of him, but obviously hadn't gotten it. Coop wouldn't be taking him out for hamburgers if they no longer needed him. They'd have already put a bullet in his head if they'd gotten what they wanted.

"You're being mighty quiet back there," Coop said in between songs, while the weatherman on the radio called for rain.

"Thinking."

"Don't hurt yourself."

He would need to seize control of the situation, which

meant getting the jump on Coop. He closed his eyes and concentrated. An image of Coop finally came together against the canvas of his eyelids. Getting the jump on Coop, with his coke-bottle glasses and anorexic physique, wouldn't have been a problem for Martin Zolotow on any other day. At the moment, however, he wasn't sure he could swat a fly. But he'd have to think of something.

There were other things he remembered. An Igloo cooler. A Cadillac. And something about Debbie. She was in some kind of danger. He could only guess that she was probably insurance against his telling Coop and the others what they wanted to know.

The Bronco slowed down and, a second later, turned off the main highway. Coop switched off the radio, for which Zolotow was immeasurably grateful. If there was to be a chance to gain control of the situation, Zolotow knew it would be soon. He flexed his right knee, wincing at the pain. It wasn't broken, but he wasn't going to be running anywhere. He'd be lucky just to walk for a few days. He probed at his ribs. There were a couple that might be cracked, but he didn't think any were actually broken. His probing fingers found something else, in his shirt pocket. A photograph. He pulled it out, wiped off the mud and studied it in the faint light from the dashboard. It was a picture of Debbie, sleeping in a hammock. They'd given it to him to prove how vulnerable she was, how easily they could reach her.

A couple things turned over in his mind. First, he'd put Debbie on the plane this morning. They'd had time, between then and now, to follow her from L.A. to Dallas, take the picture, and get it here — wherever *here* was. That spoke of proximity. He was somewhere fairly close to Dallas, definitely not still in California. San Antonio perhaps. He had friends in San Antonio. He supposed he might even be in the Dallas-Fort Worth area. There were a couple ex-cops in Dallas who owed him favors.

Second, they didn't know about his memory dysfunction — or they didn't care. That wasn't exactly something he'd been able to use to his advantage before, but he was grasping at straws, clinging to what little information he had. His life depended on his landing on his feet in the next few minutes. Scratch that. Landing on his feet *now*. The Bronco's brakes squealed as the vehicle came to a halt.

Coop turned and looked back between the seats, his face ghostly in the moonlight. "Picnic time, Zolo." He drew a revolver from under his jacket and showed it to the detective. "It's not as lethal as that injection would have been," he joked, "but it works a lot faster. Understand? You don't try anything funny. We're going to get out and walk over to the bathrooms. I'm going to let you clean up a bit. Then we're going to come back here. If the mosquitoes aren't too bad, we'll sit at a picnic table and eat our burgers. Get some fresh air." He made a face. "I need it after smelling you for the last two hours."

Zolotow tried to smile. His busted lips cracked and hurt like hell.

Coop motioned with the gun. "Come on. Sit up."

"Can't."

"Try again."

Zolotow got his arms under him and tried to lever himself up against the back of the seat. Something grabbed his lower back and crushed the muscles there. A razor blade made tick marks on his spinal column. He cried out.

"Shit. Don't tell me Billy Ray broke your fucking back." Coop reached back with his free hand and jerked the big man up to a sitting position. "I'm coming around to open the door," Coop said.

(Zolotow's fickle memory belched up a comment he'd made earlier in the day about the Bronco having no door handles in the back. A couple other tidbits fell out of the dark corners in his mind. He'd been told to get out and talk to the huge black man in the Cadillac. Tobias Weatherford Washington. There was something, too, about Bert and Ernie, those two lovable characters from Sesame Street — only that wasn't quite right. He had one of the names wrong or something, and when did Sesame Street characters start carrying Uzis?)

"Don't try anything funny."

"Wouldn't dream of it," Zolotow replied.

Coop opened the door and quickly caught the big detective as he tumbled out. "Can you stand?"

"I'm standing now, aren't I?"

"No. You're hanging on me. God, you're heavy."

Coop half carried, half dragged Zolotow down a sidewalk, through dark, wind-tossed trees, to a small brick structure. One side of the building said MEN and the other said WOMEN. Zolotow could smell it from twenty feet away. He realized at that moment that human shit smells a lot worse than cow manure.

The bathrooms might have been nice about twenty years ago. Now, the cinder-block walls were yellowed, peeling scabs. The ceiling was home to black widows and a thick accumulation of webs. Mud-daubers had built nests there to rival the greatest accomplishments of the Army Corps of Engineers. Insects scurried away across the floor when the two men entered. There was animal feces in one corner — at least Zolotow hoped it was animal feces. There were several empty bottles of cheap wine. The door wouldn't close all the way, catching in its warped frame. The two toilets were clogged and overflowing. There was no paper. The hot, stagnant air inside was thick with flies and stench. But the water was running, even if the sinks looked as if they'd been used as urinals.

Zolotow removed his shirt, moved Debbie's picture to his jean's pocket, and washed the shirt out in the sink. Most of the mud came out, and the cow manure, but the blood stains remained.

Coop stood to one side, holding his nose. "My God, Zolo, where'd you get all those fucking scars?" he asked in a high-pitched squeal. "What's that one? Twenty-two?"

"Nail gun."

"No shit?"

"No shit."

There was a dark purple bruise across his ribs. Another across his lower back. Washing the dried blood from his face, he discovered his lips were busted and there was a cut over one eye. He held his head under the cold water — though his back screamed in agony from that position — and let it ease some of the throbbing in his skull.

"Hurry up," said Coop. "Burgers are getting cold out there."

He brushed his wet hair back from his face and blinked at himself in the mirror. His nose was swollen. His eyes were bloodshot. He couldn't put all his weight on his right leg, but nothing was broken. All in all, he hadn't come out of it that badly. "You got a comb I can borrow?"

"A comb? Shit, Zolo, we're not going to a fucking party!"

"Come on, Coop, you don't want me looking like a drowned rat." He held out his hand as if reaching for a comb, his wet shirt carelessly stretched from that hand back to the other.

"You can comb your fucking hair outside," Coop snapped. "It smells like an outhouse in here." Pleased with this bit of humor, Coop chuckled. The gun wavered, and that's when Zolotow whipped it up in the sopping wet shirt. He twisted, using the sink to provide the balance his damaged knee could not, and drew Coop's arm across his hip, snapping it so hard that the revolver popped free and spun away.

Coop yelped and pulled back. Zolotow allowed the shirt to slip free, then popped Coop across the face with it. Coop's glasses flew across the room, pinged off one of the stall doors and splashed into a toilet. Zolotow whipped the shirt over Coop's head and yanked him forward. Wrapping the blinded man's head in a bear hug, he put it through the mirror, then brought it down across the porcelain sink. Coop went limp, but before he lost his grip on the bastard, Zolotow smashed his face into the sink once more for good measure. Then he let the limp man fall to the floor. Zolotow's knee went out from under him and he let himself sit down on top of the unconscious kidnapper.

"'We are not now that strength which in old days moved earth and heaven,'" he quoted, panting, "'that which we are, we are one equal temper of heroic hearts, made weak by time and fate, but strong in will to strive, to seek, to find, and not to yield.'" He slapped the unconscious man on the back of the head. "That's Tennyson, Coop. One of my favorites. Don't expect you and your redneck buddies read much though."

He sat there for a minute, catching his breath, listening to the crickets outside. An owl hooted and at least one car cruised by without stopping. Finally, he crawled over to where Coop's revolver had slid into the corner. It was a Smith and Wesson Model 66, .357 Magnum. Zolotow checked to make sure it was loaded, then he crawled back over and used the sink to pull himself to his feet. He plugged the sink and turned on the water. He leaned against the wall to one side and waited. The sink filled and ran over, pouring cold water on Coop's head. Coop sputtered and choked and sat up, nearly cracking his skull on the underside of the sink.

"You broke one of my goddamn teeth!" When he looked up, Zolotow saw that one of the teeth that had been filed to make him look like a vampire had indeed been broken off.

"You're going to answer some questions for me," Zolotow told him.

"You broke my tooth!" Coop's ghost eyes flashed in the fluorescent light of the restroom. His chin was coated with blood. He looked more devil than man.

"Shut up." Zolotow gave him a sharp tap on the top of the head with the barrel of the .357. "I've got some questions and you're going to answer them."

"I'm not telling you shit, Zolo."

"Fine." He cocked the revolver and took aim on Coop's knee.

"Wait!" Coop covered his knee with his hands, as if he thought that might stop the bullet. "Give me a minute to think about this."

"No thinking necessary," Zolotow replied. "You answer my questions or I blow your kneecap across the room. If that doesn't work, we proceed to the other knee. If necessary, we do both elbows. And if that doesn't work, I'll just give up on getting anything out of you and blow your fucking head off."

"Just a minute. I can't even see. Where are my glasses?"

Zolotow smiled. "Stall to your left, I think."

"Be a pal and get 'em for me, would ya, Zolo?"

"No fucking way."

Coop started to get up, but Zolotow rapped him with the revolver again. "Stay down there on your knees." Coop crawled over to the stall, retching at the stench. Halfway there, he paused and squinted at the grime on his hands. "Oh, God," he moaned.

"Get on with," Zolotow grumbled.

Coop crawled to the rim of the bowl, his hand clamped over his nose and mouth, his eyes running. He squinted into the commode. He uttered a helpless whimper and reached in, drawing his hand back at the last moment. "Can I go outside and find a stick?"

"No."

"Christ, Zolo, give me a break here."

"Which leg do you want it in?"

"Shit. Damn. Fuck." Coop reached into the brown soup in the commode, cussing all the while. Zolotow heard him groping around. The contents of the bowl slapped sluggishly at the porcelain. "Oh, God, they sank to the bottom."

"Hurry up."

Finally, Coop withdrew his hand, dripping shit and scraps of toilet paper, and held up his glasses. Behind the hand he had clamped over his mouth and nose, he was retching. Tears were streaming from his eyes. He came crawling on his knees out of the stall, the glasses held way out in front of him. Pureed shit ran down his wrist and stained his shirt sleeve.

"I'll kill you for this, Zolo. I'll fucking kill you. I swear I will." He crawled to the sink. "Mind if I wash these off?"

Using the wall for support, Zolotow moved away from the sink so Coop could wash off his glasses. When Coop had them planted back on his nose, his magnified eyes blinking hatred at the detective, Zolotow placed the muzzle of the gun against his head and said, "No more fucking around. Where are we?"

"What? Is that the best question you can come up with? You break my goddamn tooth, near about break my whole fucking jaw, just so you can ask where we are? I already told you once, Zolo. We just left Woodward. Up the road a piece is May and then Slapout and then Elmwood and then we'll be in Beaver."

"What state, dumbass? What state are we in?"

"You got a lot of nerve calling *me* a dumbass!" Coop turned as if there was someone else in the bathroom with them. "Fellow don't even know what fucking state he's in, and he's calling me a dumbass."

"Answer me!" Zolotow bellowed.

"Oklahoma, ya dipshit. Where'd ya think you were?"

Most of it came back to him. The airport in L.A. Earl and Billy Ray. Ernie and Bubba. Tobias Weatherford Washington. Some bullshit about vampires. McDevitt and Washington's daughter.

"You mind if I get up now?" Coop asked. "This floor's covered with God knows what."

"Stay where you are." He punctuated his instruction by tapping Coop on the forehead with the muzzle of the gun. "Who's in Dallas keeping an eye on Debbie?"

"Washington's gonna kill me if I tell you things you ain't supposed to know."

"At least he'll do it quick. If you don't answer me, I'm going to make you suffer for a long time. Piss me off and I'll shove your ugly face in the toilet."

Coop debated. Finally, Zolotow reached down and ripped the crucifix from his ear.

"Ah!" Coop squealed, grabbing his bloody ear. "What'd you do that for?"

"Answer me! Who's watching Debbie?"

"Some guy Washington uses for things down there. Used to be a professional wrestler, but now he just does wet work. Calls himself Bruiser. I don't know his real name."

But Bruiser's not there, thought Zolotow. Not if he brought those pictures up from Dallas. "How long would it take to get to Dallas from here?" he asked. "Where'd you say we were?"

"Shit, how many times you going to ask me that question? We're up near the panhandle." He drew a rough outline of Oklahoma in the slime on the floor, then made an X with his finger. "You are here, motherfucker."

"How long?"

"To Dallas? I dunno. It's about an hour and a half back to OKC. About three and a half hours from there to Dallas. Five hours. Maybe closer to four if you hauled ass and didn't get stopped by the highway patrol."

Zolotow frowned. Coop reached out as if to take back his earring, and Zolotow tossed it into the toilet where it vanished with a *plop!* into the brown sludge.

"Asshole," muttered Coop.

"How far to the nearest phone?"

"That'd be back in Woodward. About fifteen minutes, I guess."

"Let's go then. Get up." He backed off, still using the wall for support.

Coop got to his feet. "Mind if I wash my hands?" He held them up so Zolotow could see just how disgusting they were.

"Make it fast. Wash all that blood off your chin while you're at it."

While Coop did that, Zolotow tried to pull his wet shirt back on. Between having to keep the gun trained on Coop and the knives in his side, it was impossible. He wound up just tossing the shirt on the floor.

"Let's go." He motioned for the door.

"You want to lean on me, buddy?"

"Just get moving."

Coop tried to look insulted. "I was just trying to help."

"Move!"

"Sheesh."

"And the first thing we're going to do is change radio stations," Zolotow growled.

"You've got no taste, Zolo." Coop pushed open the door and stepped out into the warm night. Zolotow pushed away from the wall and hopped after him. If Coop were to try and make a run for it, Zolotow knew he'd be facing a tough decision. There was no way he could catch the man. It would come to either shooting him in the back or letting him go.

There was no need to make that decision, though. As they stepped from the bathroom, shotgun barrels were leveled from both sides of the door. Zolotow quickly debated his options as the shotguns moved to within inches of his head, but there really weren't any. Someone took the .357 from his hand. Someone else pulled his hands behind his back and secured them with duct tape. The same was done to Coop.

The two men were nondescript, what Zolotow was beginning to think of as your basic Okie. Boots. Blue jeans. Silver belt buckles. Hats. One of them had a wad of tobacco the size of a Volkswagen in his lower lip.

"Hey, come on, guys!" Coop protested. "I haven't been gone that long, have I?" Their captors didn't bother to answer him.

Zolotow and Coop were pushed toward a black sedan parked just behind the Bronco. When Zolotow fell, the two with the shotguns grabbed him by the arms and dragged him. The trunk of the sedan was opened and both men were thrown inside. A second later, over Coop's protests, the trunk was slammed shut. The sedan growled to life and accelerated away.

"One of us," Coop grumbled, "smells like shit."

"These are McDevitt's men?" Zolotow asked.

"Yeah," came Coop's answer out of the heat and the darkness and the stench.

"Where are they taking us?"

"Duh! The obvious place would be Beaver," Coop sneered, "to see McDevitt."

Zolotow wrestled with the tape on his wrists, but there was no way he was going to be able to get free. Even if he'd been strong enough to break the tape, every time he strained against it, it felt like his cracked ribs were about to puncture a lung. "You'd better start telling me some things," he told Coop.

"Save your breath, Zolo. We've got about an hour. You keep running your trap and we'll run out of air in this damn trunk. That's if the heat doesn't kill us."

"You're supposed to be one of them, but they're treating you the same as me. What gives? And how'd they know we were coming?"

Coop took a minute to think about that. "Somebody had to have tipped them off. Somebody in Washington's organization. McDevitt must think I'm setting him up."

"Well, you are. Aren't you?"

"Maybe."

"Maybe?"

"Well, maybe I'm really setting Washington up."

"Are you?"

"I dunno," Coop said. "I haven't decided yet."

"Might be a good idea if you figured it out in the next hour or so, don't you think?"

"Either way, *you're* screwed."

"Then you shouldn't have any problem answering some questions for me. Let's start with who Washington and McDevitt are. What's their racket? What's all this shit about vampires?"

Coop let out a long sigh. His breath reeked. Even over the stench of the cow manure and the residue of Coop's bathroom excursion, the man's breath was potent. "All right. What do you think of when you think of Oklahoma, Zolo?"

"Rednecks," Zolotow answered promptly.

Coop snorted. "Exactly. You think we're a bunch of down home country boys, sitting around listening to Garth Brooks and sipping moonshine. On weekends we go out and round up some outta state campers and make 'em squeal like pigs. Our women don't look much better'n our cows, and our kids all start dipping at about the age of three. Right?"

Zolotow shrugged, but the gesture was lost in the darkness. "Something like that. Can't say as I've ever been to a state yet, though, that didn't have at least some beautiful women in it."

Cooper chuckled. "You got me there. Oklahoma's got its share, Zolo. You probably won't live long enough to meet any of them, though." He shifted in the dark. "What you don't think of when you think of Oklahoma is organized crime. I tell you what, though, we've got our share of crooked politicians and cops on the take. We've got our share of drug dealers and pimps and ... You get the picture. The other thing you don't think about is high tech stuff. Oklahoma produces beef and crude oil and farm goods, right? Good old boy stuff. Ain't nobody opening a big computer chip company or genetic engineering research center in Oklahoma."

"Might be able to provide better restrooms in your picnic areas if you did."

"Ha!"

They both laughed for a minute.

"Look," Coop said, finally, "thing is, all that hillbilly stereotyping is bullshit. Oklahoma's got more diversity than your average blowhard from California thinks. And we got some mighty sharp people ... some of whom happen to be on the wrong side of the law. Washington and McDevitt are both into designer drugs."

"This is all about drugs?" Zolotow asked. "How absolutely fucking mundane. I left California for this?"

"Well, yes ... and no. McDevitt's into something else. Several something elses, actually. A couple of those something elses require women. Live women. It just so happens, he likes attractive, young black women. There's reasons for this, but you don't need to know any more. It also just so happens, one of the women he nabbed is Washington's daughter. The irony of it is that Washington used to kidnap women in OKC and sell them to McDevitt. I'd drive down and pick them up." Zolotow suddenly remembered the chains in the floorboards of the Bronco. "Washington had kinda fell behind in meeting McDevitt's needs, so I nabbed a few girls on my own. One of those was Washington's daughter."

"But McDevitt doesn't know she's Washington's daughter?"

"No. He doesn't know. Anyway, I don't think that he knows. Hell, I didn't know at first."

The car slowed down and took a sharp right turn.

"Shit. That'd be the turn onto Highway 270 at Elmwood," Coop said. "We've got about twenty minutes."

"You figured out whose side you're on?" Zolotow asked him. "You figured out what you're going to tell McDevitt?"

"If I want to live, I'd better be on McDevitt's side for the moment," Coop replied.

Zolotow could imagine his pale face screwed tight with concentration, the capillaries in his cheeks all swollen and purple. Thinking might not be his strong suit. "Here's the deal. Here's what we tell McDevitt. Washington hired you to infiltrate McDevitt's operation —"

"That ought to get me killed in the first few minutes we're there. You can count on me not going along with that story line."

"No. Listen. You and I go way back. You called me. I came out to California to pick up the cooler —"

"What's in that damn cooler?"

"Quit interrupting me. We gotta work this out, and we don't have much time. Washington hired you to infiltrate McDevitt's operation. Only you called me cause we're old pals. You and I got together in California and brought the cooler back. We were bringing the cooler to McDevitt, only Washington's goons intercepted us. We took one hell of a beating at their hands."

"That much of the story we'll have the evidence to support."

"I managed to get the drop on them, though, and we escaped."

"And whoever tipped off McDevitt that we were on our way was merely trying to ruin your reputation with him?"

"Something like that."

"What was his motivation? Let's say it's Earl or Billy Ray secretly working for McDevitt. If he's on the same side as you, why try to set you up for a fall?"

"Well, whoever it is, he's pretending to be working for McDevitt, but he's really Washington's man, so he's setting me up. Hell, every cocksucker I know's looking to stab everyone else in the back anyway. You know what they say about honor among thieves."

"That's thin, Coop."

"I'm open to suggestions."

They lay in the dark for several minutes, sweating.

"You're forgetting something," Zolotow finally said.

"Several somethings would be my guess. Which something are you referring to?"

"Our little scene in the restroom. Your broken tooth and foul odor. My holding a gun on you when they found us. How will you explain that?"

When the trunk opened, the air that rushed in was worse than the air they'd been breathing.

"What is that stench?" Zolotow asked.

"Sorry, shoulda warned you," Coop replied. "Welcome to McDevitt's hog farm."

"Hog farm?"

"Only two things this part of the state's famous for, Zolo, hogs and cow chip tossing."

"Cow chip tossing? Never mind! I don't even want to know."

"You just keep your mouth shut," Coop hissed. "Let me do all the talking. You pop off with your usual smartass comments around here and we're both dead men."

One of the shotgun brothers hauled them both, unceremoniously, out of the trunk. It must have been midnight by now. (They had taken Zolotow's wrist watch.) The night sky was moonless and overcast. All Zolotow could make out was a series of buildings hunkered down against the dark skyline. There were lights on in one, a big ranch house looking affair. In addition to the black sedan, there were several pickup trucks in the front yard, a filthy Mercedes that might have once been white, and the Bronco which Coop had driven up from OKC. While Coop walked on shaky legs, Zolo was dragged through the front yard and dumped on the steps leading up to a wide front porch that spanned the entire front of the house. Something blew against his leg and then, a second later rolled away. It was a tumbleweed, the first one Zolotow had ever seen. He watched it roll across the yard, ricochet off the corner of a barn, and disappear in the night.

Up on the dark porch, a cigarette glowed bright orange. "You got some explaining to do, Coop."

"Things ain't like they seem, boss."

The glowing butt bounced down the steps, stopping at Coop's feet. "Never are," said the disembodied voice.

Zolotow refrained from making a Smokey the Bear comment. There was something to be said about not going around irritating Oklahoma gangsters. The ones he'd met thus far had been severely lacking in humor appreciation.

Coop ground out the cigarette butt with his lizard skin boots. It was the first time Zolotow had noticed the boots. Had it not been for the shit smeared across the toes, they'd have been real attractive footwear. He made a note to ask Coop where he'd bought them — just before he broke the guy's neck, of course.

"Which one of 'em was it called you?" Coop asked. "Was it that lowlife Billy Ray? Was it Earl? I'll kill that son of a bitch."

"Never mind who called. Start talking. Start with who this guy is. Why's he laying there without no shirt, all covered in mud and cow shit? Looks like somebody done opened one helluva can of whupass on him."

"And don't think I'm going to forget it," Zolotow grumbled. One of the shotgun brothers stepped forward and thumped him in the back with the butt of his gun. Zolotow cried out.

"Easy," said the man on the porch. "Let's hear what Brother Cooper has to say first."

Coop straightened his glasses best as he could with his shoulder and cleared his throat. "Well, I went to California like you said. You were right, Jimmy, that's where Beauchamps ran off to."

Beauchamps? Zolotow looked up from the porch steps. Who the hell was Beauchamps? Something ticked in the back of his mind. Something he'd read the day before in the paper and ought to remember, but he couldn't. For a second it was close, it was right there on the tip of his tongue, then it was gone.

"You brought him back?"

Coop shook his head. "No, sir. That's not what you said for me to do. I killed the stupid nigger, just like you said. Don't worry, though, I brought back what you needed. And I brought back the other thing, too. You were absolutely right. There ain't nothing that ain't for sale in California."

"Where is it?"

"There's an Igloo in the back of the Bronco. Everything's

there, packed in dry ice."

"Good." The man on the porch leaned forward and, for a brief moment, some of the light from one of the windows touched his face. He was as pale as Coop. Completely hairless. A big, round baby face set atop a bulldog neck. "Now, who is this?" He pointed down at the steps. Then, leaning back into the shadows, he disappeared again.

"This is Martin Zolotow, a private eye from California. He's an old friend."

"That's not what I hear. I hear he was sent to kill me."

Actually, I was just sent to rescue someone's daughter, Zolotow wanted to say. *And that against my will. But you go with whatever the current lie is. I'm having trouble keeping up.*

"Well, yeah," Coop said, and it was obvious he missed having his hands to talk with. "That was the original plan ... but Zolo's an old friend of mine. We go way back. I saved his life a couple times and he owes me, see? So, I called last week to tell him I'm going to be out in L.A. We hadn't seen each other in years, ya know? I thought it would be great to get together and have a few beers. Do some reminiscing."

"Just what would the two of you be reminiscing about?"

"Huh?"

"What would you have to reminisce over, Coop? Tell me about the great times you used to have with your good buddy Zolotow there."

"That would be all the years I was a cop," Zolotow interjected. "All the years I kept trying to put Coop's sorry ass behind bars."

"That was before we got to be friends," Coop added. "Before we started working together on both sides of the law. Before I moved here," Coop said hastily, "to Oklahoma, and we lost touch with one another." He worked at the broken tooth with his tongue, nervous. And showing it.

"Go on," said the man on the porch.

"Okay. Well, see, Zolo didn't even know I was living in Oklahoma, but when I told him, he says, 'Funny you should mention Oklahoma, cause I just got a call from someone there who wants me to do something for him.' Seems that Washington wanted Zolo to fly in and do you."

"Do me?"

"Yeah. Take you out of the picture, boss. You know."

Zolotow's heart stopped. *I'm dead*, he thought. *I'm fucking dead*.

"I thought you said your friend was a private detective?"

"Well, yeah, but a guy's gotta eat, Jimmy." Coop nudged Zolotow with his lizard skin boot. "Look at the scars on this old cuss, boss. You don't think he got those taking pictures of husbands out cheating on their wives, do you? This old boy's been around the block, done more'n his share of wet work."

"So he was sent here to kill me?"

"That's what Washington thinks. But Zolo told me the whole story in L.A. Naturally, once he found out that me and you was tight, he decided not to take the job for Washington. Instead, he came here, hoping he could maybe get a job with us. Seems the heat around him in California has been building some since I was there. He's looking for a change of venue. Funny how things work out, ain't it, boss?"

The man on the porch grunted.

"Anyway, we got here, planning on bringing you the cooler and the news about Washington, but those goons Earl and Billy Ray jumped us. Poor Zolo took a hell of a beating 'fore I got the upper hand. Earl and Billy Ray run off. I wanted to go after them..." Coop looked down at Zolo with mock affection. "...for Zolo's sake, mind you, but I figured I'd better get that cooler to you straightaway."

"Smart thinking."

"So, which one of them was it? Was it Earl or Billy Ray what called you and told you lies about me?"

"Neither," said the man on the porch. Boards creaked and a chair back thumped against the wall of the house. The man stepped forward into the light. He was a good seven feet tall. Bald as an egg. Built like Hulk Hogan. He was wearing overalls with nothing on underneath, and his flesh was as pale as a dead fish. When he smiled, he revealed that his canines had been filed down, same as Coop's. "Toby himself called me a couple hours ago."

"Toby Washington?"

"Yeah." Jimmy McDevitt came down the steps, which creaked and protested under his weight. "He made me a deal. Offered to sell the identity of a backstabbing traitor and a hit man if I would release some nigger girl. Said he was a friend of her family, how he'd like to see her sent back home to Oak City." McDevitt thumped Coop in the center of his chest, knocking him over on his ass. "He said you were going to sell me out, Coop. Said your buddy here was going to put a bullet in my head."

"That's a lie, Jimmy! Hell, I'm one of your own. We've hunted coon together, man!" Sweat ran from Coop's black, greasy hair, trailing down his pasty cheeks. He was trembling.

McDevitt took a shotgun from one of the two men in the yard and placed the barrel against Coop's head, knocking his glasses askew. "I'm sorry it had to come to this, Coop."

"Christ, Jimmy, don't do this! I'm one of your own, man!" Coop was bawling now. "Look at me, Jimmy! I got maybe three months to live on account of that shit you shot me up with. Why would I want to kill you? You're my only chance for a cure, man. Oh, God, Jimmy, I'd die for you, man. Please don't —"

McDevitt steadied the shotgun. "Nobody betrays me and lives."

"I didn't. I swear to God, I didn't, Jimmy. You look in that cooler, man. I did everything you said. I brought what you asked for. Please don't kill me."

McDevitt looked to Zolotow. "What about this big ugly son of a bitch?"

"Look who's talking," Zolotow replied.

The shotgun shifted. "Any reason I should spare him, too?"

"Just don't kill me," Coop begged. "I don't give a fuck what you do with him."

"Thanks, Coop," Zolotow muttered.

McDevitt pointed the shotgun at Zolotow. "What's your

real story, asshole?"

"Coop told you already, egghead."

"You got balls," McDevitt chuckled. "I'll give you that much."

"They're about the only thing Earl and Billy Ray didn't break," Zolotow replied.

McDevitt grinned. "So I see." He looked to his henchmen. "You say they were trying to kill each other on the way here?" The men nodded. "Somebody want to explain that to me?" McDevitt asked, directing the question to no one in particular.

"I'd changed my mind," Zolotow answered quickly, before Coop could dig them a deeper hole. "Decided that Coop was pulling my leg. He wouldn't tell me what the hell you were up to out here in the boonies. Kept saying you were raising pigs, but I knew it had to be more than that. I told him this whole thing was starting to smell pretty bad. I told him I was going to take Washington's offer, cause at least I knew his money was good."

"You telling me this so I'll spare your life?" McDevitt snickered. "You think you can walk away after telling me you were going to kill me?"

"I'm telling you this because I think you're a man who respects the truth," Zolotow lied.

"Just kill the cocksucker," Coop suggested.

"Shut up," McDevitt told him. "Is that any way to talk to your old friend?" He looked back to Zolotow. "So, you were going to come in here, all busted up like that, and take me out?"

"I might have gone back to L.A. and rested a week or two first. Washington didn't set any specific deadlines. But I'd have come back," Zolotow said, "and paid you a visit."

"And killed me?"

"Depends." Zolotow grinned. "You might have made me a better offer for Washington's head."

"Hmm. Yeah, I might have." He handed the shotgun to his henchman. "Take the private eye out in the barn and tie him up."

"You're not gonna kill him?" asked Coop. He sounded

disappointed.

"Maybe later." McDevitt signaled the second henchman. "Bring Brother Cooper in the house and help him get cleaned up. I ain't sure what to do with him, but he's still one of our own. And send someone out after that cooler."

Pigs had recently been at the straw. Zolotow could smell them. It wasn't as bad as the fumes outside, but, still, he could tell, there'd been pigs in this barn. Once again, he'd been left in the dark. He could make out the dim outline of saddles and farm equipment in the starlight coming in through windows up in the loft. There might be tools with which he could manipulate an escape, but his ankles had been taped together, same as his wrists. McDevitt bought only the finest in duct tape. Zolotow wasn't going anywhere.

He was alone in the dark with his thoughts, left to ponder the things he knew about today's bizarre events and to wonder what he'd forgotten that might help it all make sense.

So you've got this pig farmer in the Oklahoma panhandle making designer drugs. And, oh, by the way, the guy thinks he's a vampire. He's got other vampire followers, including Zolotow's old friend Coop. For some reason, they need young, black women. What for? Well, maybe they use them to make the drugs. Indian women in the jungles of Mexico are used to make and package cocaine for sale to the United States. Why not use black women in a lab to make designer drugs? Cause it didn't make any sense. These are designer drugs, the manufacture of which ought to require some level of laboratory skills. The vampire bit didn't make sense either. And the Licking Valley Coon Hunters Club? What was that all about? This was Beaver, Oklahoma, home of the World Championship Cow Chip Tossing Contest, not Licking Valley.

And just what was in that damn cooler?

Who was Beauchamps?

And —

"Psst."

Zolotow lifted his head from the straw.

"You awake?" someone whispered.

It was a woman's voice. Zolotow tried to place its location. It seemed to be coming from the other side of the barn's outside wall.

"Hey. Can you hear me?"

"Who are you?" Zolotow asked.

"Kendra."

"Where are you, Kendra?"

"Outside. I can just barely see you through this crack in the wall. Are you hurt?"

"I've had better days. Listen, can you get in here?"

"There's a lock on the door."

"Where's the key? Is there another way in? I really need your help, Kendra."

"If I help you, will you help me?"

"If I can. What do you want me to do?"

"Get me out of here. Take me home. Before —" She hesitated. "Before it's my turn."

"Your turn for what?"

"For ... the hunt."

Interlude: "Explain this theory of yours to me."

"It's a theory about beauty and women," Zolotow told Dr. Mary Ellis. She was wearing a beige satin skirt that hugged her hips, topped off with a matching jacket and a blue blouse. When she'd walked between him and the sunlight pouring in through her office's full-length window, he'd noticed that she wasn't wearing underwear. He suspected that she'd purposely taken that stroll around her desk and past the window. Whether she thought she could distract him enough to let something slip or whether this was but one phase in an ultimate seduction, he couldn't say. She was crafty. Much more intelligent than the women he was used to dealing with. And as hard and frozen as an ice cube. No doubt about it, she'd sleep with him if it served her purpose. Fascinating, but his sessions with her continued to reinforce the fact that he definitely did not want to start a relationship with her.

"It's possible," he said, continuing with the explanation of his theory, "easy, in fact, to find something beautiful about every woman. The hands of this one. The way that one's eyes light up when she smiles. Her laugh. A neck. The ankles. Calves and thighs and hips. The way this one walks. Shoulder blades, throat, ribcage ... you name it. Every woman is beautiful in some way. Every woman has some element of perfection."

"Fascinating," Dr. Ellis said, perching herself on the corner of her desk. "So, you don't think there are any ugly women? All women are physically attractive? And," she cut off his retort, "for this reason you must find yourself physically attracted to every woman you meet, right?"

"I didn't say that. And, sure, there are ugly women out there. I'm reminded of a flick I watched a few weeks ago on cable with Lizelle, a comedy about bowling called *Kingpin*. Woody Harrelson and Bill Murray star in it. There's a woman in that movie, the landlord, who would certainly strain my theory." He gave the psychologist a mock shudder, curling his lips distastefully. "In fact, she might invalidate it.

"But my point is not that there aren't ugly women out there — ugly being defined as a sum total of a woman's physical appearance. My point is that there is something beautiful about every woman. All you have to do is look."

She leaned forward, her blouse gaping to reveal a low cut turquoise brassiere and the velvet cleft where her breasts were pressed together. "And you are a looker, aren't you, Detective Zolotow?"

He raised his eyes and met her gaze. "Yes, ma'am, I suppose I am. But it's more than just looking. A really beautiful woman is beautiful on the inside, too. It's her bearing, her behavior ... the way she reacts when you open a door for her or even the way she reacts when you don't. To really see the beauty in a woman, you have to look beyond her skin."

"And what do you see when you look at me, Detective Zolotow?"

He smiled and pointed over her right shoulder at the clock. "Right now, I see that our time is up, Dr. Ellis."

THREE: *Duct Tape and a Midnight Stroll — Genetics and the Grad Student — The Igloo (again) and the Stronger Sex — High Speed Pursuit and Tumbleweeds — Cop Killers and Moonbeams*

Kendra was afraid to turn on the lights in the barn for fear someone outside would see them and come to investigate. She settled for striking a few matches, by which she located Zolotow lying face down in the straw. As the match light flickered off her smooth, ebony cheeks, Zolotow saw that she was little more than a girl. Eighteen and not a day more, he guessed. Her teeth, when she smiled at him, were even and white. Her eyes were as dark as a moon-cast shadow. Her hair was shoulder length and drawn back in a knot behind her head. The match flame lent the faintest of red highlights to her hair's black luster. She had a figure most women could only dream of, displayed in cut off denim shorts and a thin halter top. She might have been a model, but he suspected she made a lot less at her current profession.

"Where'd you get the key?"

"There's a key cabinet in the lab," Kendra explained as she tugged at the duct tape on his ankles. "The lab has cipher locks, but I got the combination off one of the technicians while he was asleep. Stupid geek had it written on the palm of his hand."

Zolotow didn't have to ask how she came to be sleeping with the lab technician. Women were probably a fringe benefit in an outfit like this. "Where is this lab?"

"Big building back of the house," she replied. "You're not blind, are you? I don't think a blind guy's going to be much help to me."

"Sorry, it was already dark when I got here. I don't know the layout."

"What's your name?"

"Martin Zolotow. Why don't you check the work bench over there and see if you can find something to cut that tape. You're never going to get it off that way."

She returned a moment later with a rusty utility knife and began sawing at the thick wrapping of tape on his ankles. He groaned as she shifted his right leg. "Are you hurt?" she asked.

For a second, he debated how to answer, wondering if she'd free him if he told her the truth about his injuries. The caution in her voice masked any sign of concern. Or else she felt none. She might see him not as a victim to be rescued, but rather as a potential ally. If he was of no use to her ... well, then she might has well leave him behind. But it wasn't in his nature to lie, especially not to women. "A couple rednecks roughed me up a bit," he admitted. "One of them was a baseball fan. He tried to score a home run on my knee. You cut me loose and I'll be good to go, though."

She hesitated a second or two, probably wondering just how useful an injured man was to her. Then she sighed and went back to sawing at the tape. "What are you doing here, Martin Zolotow?"

"I was sent to find a girl."

"Yeah? Girls we've got. I think there's a whorehouse just across the Texas border that's a whole lot safer, though. I imagine they'd even do this bondage bit, you asked them nicely."

"I'll keep that in mind if I get out of this mess. How many girls are here?"

"Fourteen at the moment. Probably lose a few tomorrow or the next day though."

"To this hunt that you mentioned?"

"Yeah. McDevitt and his fucking club. Every time there's a meeting, several of us disappear. One of the girls overheard that there was a meeting tomorrow. I was thinking of making a run for it on my own, see if I could bring back help. One girl might manage to slip out, whereas all of us disappearing would be noticed pretty quick. Most of the boys working for McDevitt tend to hang around, if you know what I mean."

"I think I do."

"Anyway, I was making my great escape when I saw them drag you in here. What's that old saying about the enemy of my enemy being my friend? One way or another, I'm out of here tonight. I don't want to be here tomorrow when it's time for that meeting. I've been here too long already. My number's surely up."

"We'll see if we can do something about that." His legs popped free and Kendra moved to his wrists. "Careful you don't cut me with that," he said. "It's been a few years since I had a tetanus shot."

"From the look of these scars, you've had your share of tetanus shots in the past," she said, lightly touching his back. "Looks like you've made a habit of pissing people off. Hope you learned to quit turning your back on them afterward."

"Some of those didn't come from behind."

"Oh," she said with a pause. It hadn't occurred to her that bullets often pass right through a man. "Who are you looking for anyway?"

He realized then that no one had told him Washington's daughter's name. Coop was probably supposed to do that at some point, but Coop, like everyone else in this nightmare, seemed to have his own agenda. "I only know her last name. Washington."

"Yeah?"

His wrists parted and he was suddenly free. He rolled over and tried to sit up, but the pain in his lower back was too much. Kendra helped him.

"Do you know her?" he asked.

"We don't exchange too many last names, Martin. Could be I know her. Could be she's dead already." She struck a match so she could see his face. "Could be ... that *my* last name's Washington."

He studied her in the match light. There was an old bruise

beneath her left eye, nearly faded. Makeup would have hidden it, but she wasn't wearing any. It was the kind of bruise a hooker got for payment. "Here's your money, bitch." *Smack!* "Next time make sure you at least pretend to cum." It was the sort of thing that left permanent scars. Not scars you could see. Internal scars. The kind that don't heal. But Kendra's eyes were clear and bright. She didn't look away when he stared at her, but met and held his gaze with a frightened intensity. He understood her fear. She was afraid he either wouldn't or couldn't help her. She was afraid he was no better than the guy who'd left that bruise under her eye. She was wondering if she could trust him or if she should lie and tell him that she was the girl he was looking for. Lying, however, did not appear to be something she was comfortable with either.

The match burned down to her fingers, and she blew it out. "I don't know anyone named Washington," she said softly. "We'll check, though. If she's here, we'll find her."

"Thanks, Kendra."

She turned away, but he caught her shoulder and turned her back to face him. "Strike another match," he told her. He suspected that she understood that some things can't be said in the dark. She lit a match and he met her gaze in the orange light. "I'll get you out of here, too, Kendra. It's over. Okay?"

She swallowed and nodded. Relief, but no tears. This was not a girl who cried.

"Go back to the workbench and find a roll of that duct tape," he said, blowing out the match before it could burn her. "See if you can find a broom handle while you're at it. And, Kendra," he called after her as she crossed the barn, "anything that looks like it might make a weapon, you bring that back, too."

She returned a moment later with a roll of duct tape, a handful of paint stir sticks, and a pipe wrench. "If I'm guessing correctly at what you wanted the broom handle for, these ought to do almost as good if you double them up. And this…" she added, hefting the pipe wrench, "…was always enough weapon for my daddy. He was a plumber."

He nodded. "Hold these here while I do the taping."

While she held a pair of the flat sticks on either side of his right knee, he wrapped the knee in duct tape. By the time the roll of tape was gone, he had a thick, stiff wrapping that he could stand on. The sticks kept him from bending the knee, kept it from dropping out from under him.

Kendra helped him to his feet. He took a couple practice swings with the pipe wrench, grimacing at the pain in his side and lower back. "Don't suppose there was a gun lying around over there?"

"Just a couple of AK-47s," she replied, her teeth showing in the dark, "but I thought you'd prefer the wrench."

"Clever girl. You ready to show me the way out of here?"

The barn door looked out on the yard in front of the house. The Bronco, the Mercedes, and the pickup trucks were still parked out front. The house was completely dark. Though a sliver of a moon had come up, peeking through the heavy clouds, it was low on the horizon, behind the house. It was impossible to tell if there was anyone sitting on the dark porch, but Zolotow reasoned that Kendra had already crossed the yard without incident.

"Don't suppose you thought to look for car keys while you were in the lab?" he asked.

"I did, but there weren't any."

"I guess that really would have been too easy."

"Maybe the car keys are in the house?"

"Maybe." He leaned against the barn door and studied the house, assessing it for possible entry points. There might have been a key to the house in the lab. He thought about asking her, but the problem was that there was no way he could move quietly. He'd sound like Frankenstein's Igor trying to sneak through the silent house. He looked at Kendra, standing there in her cutoffs, her long black legs painted in moonlight. She was watching him think, waiting for him to tell her what to do. He couldn't send her into the house either.

"We need a phone," he said. "One phone call, and I can bring more shit down on this place than..." He trailed off as several drops of rain dotted her halter top. "Damn, that's all we need."

"So we try to get in the house and use a phone?"

"No. The lab. You said you had the combination. There'll be a phone there." He took her hand. "Come on."

The moist night air stank of pig shit. It was hot, suffocating and humid. The temperature might have dropped below a hundred when the sun went down, but not by much. "Is it always this stinking hot here?"

"Welcome to the panhandle, Martin."

They used the vehicles as cover crossing the yard, then slipped around the side of the house. There were lights on at the back of the house. Zolotow hesitated. "It's okay," Kendra told him, squeezing his hand. "Some of the boys are in the kitchen, drinking. They're beyond noticing us."

A low growl came out of the shadows near the back porch. Zolotow froze, raising the wrench.

"Wait," Kendra hissed. She let go of Zolotow's hand, knelt, and whispered into the darkness. "It's okay, Razor. Come here, boy. Come on."

"Razor?"

A black shape detached itself from the shadows and ran toward her. "Good boy, Razor." She took the rottweiler's head in her hands and kissed the top of his head. "Yes, you are a good guard doggy, aren't you? Kendra's bestest friend in the whole wide world. Good boy, Razor." The rottweiler buried his snout in the girl's crotch and sniffed happily, wagging most of his body.

"Now I've seen everything," Zolotow remarked.

Razor looked up at him, showed his teeth, and growled.

"Quiet, Razor." Kendra clamped her hands around the dog's snout, closing his mouth. She pressed her face close to his. "You stay right here and guard the house for me. Can you do that? Course you can. Razor's a smart doggy." She kissed him on his big black nose. "That's Kendra's good baby. Stay." Then she took Zolotow's hand and pulled him toward the large metal building behind the house. Razor watched them go, his tongue hanging.

"Helps to make friends with local security," Zolotow said.

"Oh, Razor's a real sweetheart," Kendra said. "He'd

have taken your leg off, though."

"The good one or the bad one?"

"Probably both."

Thunder rumbled in the distance and more raindrops fell. "Come on, before it really starts raining."

The rear of McDevitt's house was guarded by an ancient washing machine rusting placidly into the red dirt of the yard. Light from the kitchen windows cast the washer's shadow in a long column that fell against the side of a corrugated metal building. The lab had no windows, but from several vents up near the roof Zolotow could see that there were lights on inside. Kendra passed the front door. "We'll go in through the back, where they take deliveries. Less chance of anyone seeing us. We have to be quiet though, because there might still be someone working."

They followed the contour of the building — Zolotow estimated its size at about a hundred feet by fifty feet. Behind the building lay a vast expanse of darkness which, when lightning strobed in the distance, Zolotow saw was prairie. He believed he was looking north, but the heavy cloud cover prevented him from being certain. To the west were several other smaller buildings. In one of them, he guessed, he'd find Washington's daughter and the other girls Kendra had mentioned. To the east lay a vast series of small sheds and fences. Most of the stench seemed to be coming from that direction. Hogs. Sweet, sleeping piggies, Kendra might call them. Good little piggies guarding their slop troughs. He'd never smelled anything so awful in his life.

The rain suddenly broke lose. Zolotow leaned his head back and let the cool moisture run down his throat. He wasn't sure whether the rain would drown out the pig stench or merely stir it up and make it worse, but for the moment it didn't matter. The rain was cool and refreshing. Where it trailed across his countless bruises and lacerations, it left a soothing wake, proving that he wouldn't always have to hurt as bad as he did now. When he looked back at his companion, her shirt had soaked through. The halter top clung to her like a second layer of skin. In the dark, she looked as topless as he was.

"This way," whispered Kendra, leading him around the

corner where they nearly collided with a young black man.

Zolotow raised the wrench. The young man raised a crowbar. For a few seconds, they both stood there, like gladiators about to start hacking away at each other in the night. The rain came down in a torrent and lightning split the night. Zolotow blinked the rain from his eyes. He lowered the pipe wrench. "Crowbars are probably not standard issue for McDevitt's goons," he said softly, his voice nearly lost in the rumbling of thunder.

"Neither are pipe wrenches."

Zolotow nodded. "So, we've both proven ourselves to be thinking men. I'm glad we didn't start whaling away at each other. What are you doing here?"

"I could ask you the same thing," said the man with the crowbar.

Zolotow shrugged. "Martin Zolotow, kidnapping victim, having the worst day of my life, and this rain just tops it off. This is Kendra, and she'd appreciate it if you quit staring at her as if she was naked."

The young black man swallowed. "Sorry." He extended a hand. "Daryl Johnson."

He was clean-shaven, with soft, handsome features and intelligent eyes — none of the rough-edges that Zolotow was used to seeing in the mirror. He was short and thin, in khaki Dockers, mud-covered loafers, and a polo shirt that might have been dark blue or green, but now looked black in the downpour. His hair was cut close to his scalp, beading with water. "I'm a grad student from O.U."

"A what?"

Kendra took Johnson's hand. "Kendra Wilkes. Nice to —"

"Do you have a cell phone?" Zolotow asked him. "A car?"

"I've got a rental car parked a mile down the road. I didn't want anyone to see it."

"That's it then," Zolotow said, "we're out of here."

"No way!" Johnson protested. "I didn't come all the

way out here to leave without seeing what's in this lab."

"Look, I don't think you understand what you're getting yourself in to," Zolotow told him. "This ain't your average hog farm. That stench is what your criminal elements call a cover up operation, my young friend."

"I know that." Johnson wrinkled his nose. "And speaking of stench, what have you been wallowing in anyway?" He leaned closer in the rain. "Shit! Are all those scars?"

"Look, kid, I'm not gonna stand here in the rain and debate this with you. We're all going to pile in your car and get the hell out of here. The boys that run this place aren't the kind of people a nice college boy wants to hang out with."

Johnson showed him the crowbar. "I didn't come here to visit. I came to break in. I'm not leaving before I get a look in this lab. If you think you can find my car, you just head off down the road and take a look for yourself. I'll be along shortly."

The kid had spunk. And Zolotow was in no shape to deal with him without someone getting hurt. "Okay. No sense standing out here in the rain all fucking night." Zolotow pushed past him and limped to the delivery entrance.

"Seven. Six. Nine. Two," said Kendra.

"You have the number?" exclaimed Johnson.

Zolotow punched it in and was rewarded with a click from the lock. He cautiously pulled open the door, peering inside. In the light that spilled out, Johnson continued his appraisal of Kendra's drenched form, much to Zolotow's disapproval. The girl didn't seem to notice. It was the sort of evaluation she'd undoubtedly come to expect from men. Beyond the door was a storage area and delivery room. Except for boxes and several trash barrels, a dolly and some other junk, the room was empty. There was a phone on the far wall. Zolotow pulled his two companions in out of the rain and closed the door behind them.

He stuck a finger under Johnson's nose. "Don't move an inch." Then he crossed the room and picked up the phone. Nothing. No dial tone. No switch board. Nothing. He checked the cord. The phone was plugged in. Maybe he needed to dial a nine or something for a line. He tried that. Tried several other combinations. Nothing.

"Well?" Kendra asked.

"It must be on a security system or something," he said disgustedly. "Probably requires a four digit code to get a line."

"Did you try using the door code?" she asked.

"Yeah. No luck. Quiet now." Zolotow eased open the door leading into the rest of the building and cautiously peered through the crack. Cold air spilled from the room, raising the damp hair on his chest, causing him to shiver.

Laboratory. There was a lot of glass. Beakers. Test tubes. Machines with which he was unfamiliar. Microscopes. Autoclaves. Centrifuges. Something was beeping. There were a thousand diodes flashing from instrument panels. Storage cabinets. Roll around carts covered with instruments. An eye wash rack. Panel after panel of fluorescent lights suspended from the ceiling. White lab garments on hooks along one wall. Vials and vials of chemicals racked in cabinets and tables and rollaways. There was a walk-in cooler to the right. There was a row of offices and smaller rooms to the left.

The place looked empty.

Johnson tried to peer in around Zolotow.

"I told you to stay put!"

"Shit," said Johnson. "They're actually set up to do it." Zolotow allowed the door to swing open so the grad student could see the whole lab. "This is something!"

"What are you talking about?"

"Genetic engineering." Johnson pushed his way past Zolotow. "They've got everything they need."

"Genetics? I thought they were making drugs here."

"They're set up for that, too," said Johnson. "Maybe some other things as well. Hell, there's twenty million dollars worth of equipment in this room. Not much you couldn't do with it."

Zolotow suddenly remembered Coop saying something to McDevitt about having been shot up with something. Had he been injected with something here? Was his impending demise the result of what they'd done to him in this lab?

Kendra circled the room, trying different phones. None of them gave her a dial tone. She looked to Zolotow, her face desperate, and he signaled for her to hold on. They could all hear the rain coming down on the metal roof over their heads.

"I think you'd better tell me what you're doing here," Zolotow told Johnson.

Johnson was poking at the equipment, scanning every document left out on the work benches, opening desk drawers, and nosing into everything he could. "I do work in genetic engineering," he explained. "At O.U., the University of Oklahoma in Norman." He looked up. "Sorry, I can tell from your accent that you're not from around these parts."

"Nor do I intend to remain in these parts any longer than I have to," Zolotow responded, somewhat more heatedly than he had intended. "The sooner you speed up this story…"

"Oh. Yeah. Well, about six months ago, I got a phone call from some group here in Beaver. They wanted some information, wanted me to verify some test results. For about four months, we worked some things out over the phone and by email, making some real breakthroughs. I tell you what, there's some real genius behind the things being done in this room. I thought we might actually be getting close, but then they suddenly quit taking my phone calls. I thought I was about to get ripped off, that McDevitt's lab was about to publish something for which I'd get no credit. I thought I'd come and see for myself." He looked at the crowbar sheepishly. "That back door was a mother though." He tossed the crowbar down on the nearest workbench.

"How'd you get past the dog?" asked Kendra.

"What dog?"

Zolotow snorted. "He snuck right past while Razor was busy having you scratch his ears, hon. That's how."

"Oh."

Zolotow turned back to Johnson. "You said they were close to something. Close to what?"

"Synthetic telomerase."

"What's that?"

"The telomere is the end segment on a strand of DNA,"

Johnson explained. "As the cell divides, the telomere shortens. It's like a clock. When the telomere is gone, the cell quits dividing. It ages. It dies. Telomerase enables the telomere to replenish itself." He stared at Zolotow as if that explained everything. When Zolotow stared back blankly, without comment, Johnson said, "Look, if we could prevent our cells from aging —"

"We could live forever," Kendra interjected.

"Well, theoretically," Johnson said, "but realistically, there are dozens of other villains waiting to strike a person down, from lipofuscin accumulation, to mitochondrial damage, to toxin accumulation, etcetera. The more practical application of this research is in curing cancer and forestalling AIDS."

"A cure for cancer?" Kendra exclaimed.

"Yeah. With cancer cells, it's just the other side of the coin. Cancer cells don't listen when they're told to quit dividing. They multiply like wildfire, spreading and killing the host. They don't obey the laws of apoptosis." He saw that he was confusing them again. "Programmed cell death," he explained. "Your genes are really only designed to support you up until you've reproduced and assured your own offspring of their chance of survival. Evolution has a vested interest in giving you a fair chance to pass on your DNA, but after that you're of little use."

While the college kid went into lecture mode, rattling off polysyllable words like only the truly over-educated could, Zolotow leaned against a cabinet and tried to think. He was struck suddenly by his reflection in cabinet's glass front. He looked like shit. He looked like yesterday's leftovers, like the proverbial something that the cat dragged in. One eye was swollen. Both were bloodshot. His lower lip was busted and the crust of dried blood there had run down his chin in the rain. His ribs were blue. Despite the downpour, he was still covered with mud and unthinkables.

"Thirty five years ago," Johnson droned on, "a researcher by the name of Leonard Hayflick found that normal cells die no matter what he did to preserve them. The prevailing belief at the time was that individual cells could live forever in the lab, but Hayflick watched cells divide a set number of times and then die.

This limit on cell life is now known as the Hayflick limit. The limit is caused by the telomere. At conception, your telomere is about ten thousand base pairs long. By birth it has already shortened to about five thousand pairs. Your cells invest half of their telomeres just to create you. If the telomere never shortened, your cells wouldn't age."

There were several strands of straw in Zolotow's hair. He plucked them out and dropped them on the floor. He was tired, he was hungry, and he was mad. Given a proper weapon and a leg that would hold him, he'd like nothing better than to kick the door down on that house. In his present condition, though, that was suicide. What he needed was to reach a friend. The phones were a dead end. He scanned the room again. He had missed something important. He was sure of it.

Johnson paused to catch a breath. Kendra slipped in, "And you can cure cancer with this?"

"We think so. Cancer and some aging disorders like Hutchinson-Gilford and Werner's syndrome, two rare progeria diseases. We can forestall AIDS, too. The reason an HIV victim gets AIDS is that his white blood cells have been lost and replaced so many times that they're no longer able to multiply. The immune system ultimately fails for lack of white blood cells. HIV causes the shortening of the telomere in the white blood cells to be accelerated. But if we could prevent the telomere from shortening, then the white blood cells would never cease replacing themselves. The person would still have the virus, HIV, but they would never develop AIDS."

"But that's not what McDevitt is using the lab for, is it?" Zolotow asked as he paced the room. "He doesn't care about curing society's ills." Zolotow was thinking of Coop's pale, smooth skin, like a newborn baby's. Some of what they were doing here might have worked, though the ultimate cost to Coop was too high. He'd said he was dying. He'd said McDevitt was his only chance for a cure.

Johnson indicated the racks of computers and equipment. "With this kind of money to throw around, I'd say he was working toward the whole enchilada. He was after immortality."

"'To hold infinity in the palm of your hand and eternity in an hour,'" quoted Zolotow.

"William Blake," said Kendra, surprising both the men.

Johnson grinned and put an arm around her wet shoulders. "It is so nice to meet an educated woman. What'd you say your name was? Kendra?"

She pried free of his arm. "How do you make this telomerase stuff? How do you administer it?"

"We don't have time for this," Zolotow told them. "We need car keys and we need them now. We need to get to a phone." But there was another way to get a message out, wasn't there? The computers!

Johnson ignored him, prattling on to Kendra. There were two approaches to adjusting the telomeric clock, he said, resetting it and stopping it. Both had been accomplished with cells in a laboratory environment.

Zolotow sat down at one of the computers. When he tapped the space bar, the screen lit up and asked him for a user name and a password. He pushed back his chair and moved on to the next one.

"The simple approach," Johnson went on, "is to add telomerase. Telomerase isn't found in most human cells, but the gene for it is present in every cell. In fact," and he placed his arm around her shoulders again, "the DNA in African-American females shows the strongest proclivity for telomerase production."

The second computer also prompted him for a user name and password. So did the third and the fourth.

"There are three ways to reset the telomere: administer either a telomerase analog, a gene that expresses telomerase, or an inducer that unlocks the human telomerase gene. A telomerase analog would be an artificial telomerase that's tougher and more durable than the real thing. Real telomerase is fragile and quickly destroyed by the normal enzymes in the blood stream. Its half life is so short that it won't work by injection."

The eighth computer Zolotow tried came up with some sort of graphic display feed from a spread spectrum analyzer. Zolotow clicked to minimize this window and behind it he found the email account for one Julio Alahandro, M.D. It was open. It was hardwired to an Internet server. He chuckled softly and clicked NEW MAIL, then typed the following address: hgarza@sapd.police.net.

"The second approach, introducing new genes into the human body so that telomerase is naturally produced, isn't yet practical. The problem is that we don't understand the full human DNA sequence."

Zolotow typed fast:

> *Hector, ignore the name at the top of this email. This is Martin Zolotow. When last we saw one another, we were sipping margaritas on your front porch. You offered me a job with SAPD and we talked about how I would not be following a certain lady friend anymore. Later, I told you over the phone how I had tracked down this lady's nemesis in France and sent her the information on where to find him. I'm telling you these things so that you will know that this is really me, Hector.*

"The third approach, perhaps the best, is to induce one's own genes to produce telomerase. Every human somatic cell already has telomerase genes; the trick is to turn them on. This," said Johnson, "is what I believe they've done here."

> *I am in Beaver, Oklahoma, and I am in deep shit. I need help, but more importantly, I need you to protect a friend of mine. Debbie Montgomery, a young lady I sent home to her parents in Dallas yesterday morning, will be hurt if I don't do something here. The man who is to hurt her is an ex-wrestler known as Bruiser. I'm sorry, it's all I have. Debbie's*

parents are Ken and Eliza Montgomery. Call back to LA, have someone break into my office, get an address, get word to them. Better yet, please, my old friend, get there yourself and make sure she is safe. I will be in touch as soon as I can — with any luck, before this email even reaches you, if I can get to a phone.

Zolotow spent several minutes trying to remember the Montgomerys' address or phone number, wanting to scroll up and add it to the message. No luck. He was surprised he was able to remember as much as he had. He hoped it was enough for Garza to go on. When he was sure he wasn't getting anywhere, he clicked SEND.

"I helped them make the breakthrough of the century," said Johnson, "and then they dropped me like a hot potato. Soon as I have proof..."

"Well," said Kendra, prying herself free of Johnson's arm once again, "I don't think you have anything to worry about, Daryl. They might have gotten close here, but these men aren't immortal. I've seen two of these Coon Hunters keel over sick in the three months I've been held here. Several others don't look to have long left. Whatever they've shot themselves up with, it's killing them."

"'As if you could kill time without injuring eternity,'" quoted Zolotow, stepping back from the computer.

When they both stared at him blankly, he smiled and said, "Thoreau." Then he took a lab coat from a rack and pulled it on. "Let's get the hell out of here."

They were halfway across the yard when the back door of the house opened and spilled a narrow band of light out into the rain.

"Freeze!" Zolotow hissed, certain that one of his startled companions would bolt. "Don't move an inch, either of you." None of them were caught directly in the light from the doorway. There wasn't a star in the sky and the moon was hidden behind clouds and downpour. The ancient washer might even be partially blocking them. As long as they didn't move, they should be invisible in the gloom. Kendra was close enough that he could grab her arm. He did so. Her skin was cold and wet. He glared at Johnson, as if by sheer will he could root the man in place.

A thin, scarecrow of a man staggered into the bright doorway. "Shit!" he exclaimed. "It's wetter'n your old lady out here, Bishop. I say to hell with the cooler. I'll get it in the morning."

Another face peered out into the night. "McDevitt will kick your sorry ass all the way back to Ohio if he finds out you forgot to bring that damn thing in like he told you, Digger. Was me, I'd haul my ass out there and get it now. Fuck the rain. You ain't gonna melt."

"Hell, *you* go get it!"

"I ain't the one was told to bring it in, dipshit. Go on now, 'fore your beer gets warm."

Bishop pushed his friend out into the rain and slammed the door shut behind him. Digger stood under the shelter of the back porch for a minute, cussing under his breath; then he reached into his pocket, pulled out a ring of keys, and stomped off through the mud toward the front yard. He was weaving, slopping through puddles without a care, his long legs as bowed and ungainly as a giraffe's. He belched loudly and scratched at his ass. Razor came out of the shadows, barking and showing his teeth. Digger told the dog to shut up. Zolotow acknowledged once again how popular that response was in Oklahoma. *Nine out of ten of your average Okies*, he thought, *use it in regular conversation at an alarming rate*. Razor watched Digger walk past; then, smelling Kendra, the rottweiler ran, slipping and sliding in the mud, straight to the young prostitute, where he buried his nose in her crotch. Zolotow acknowledged how the guard dog sure had a nose for the finer things in life.

"Good boy, Razor," Kendra cooed softly. "Razor's a good guard doggy."

"Quiet," Zolotow whispered. He set off limping through the rain after Digger. Johnson and Kendra and Razor followed.

"Slop the hogs, Digger. Fix the fence, Digger. Go out

and bring in the cooler, Digger." The man muttered a steady stream of this, punctuated with curses. "They treat me like a goddamn coon or something."

Digger went straight to the rear of the Bronco, where he proceeded to fumble with the keys. Zolotow and company slipped in behind one of the trucks, just twenty feet away. Zolotow hefted the pipe wrench and braced himself to move, but his side and back hurt so bad, he didn't think he could take the man down quickly enough. He couldn't afford to give Digger time to cry out or go for a weapon. Zolotow grabbed the grad student and pulled him close, pushing the wrench into his hands. "When he bends over to put the keys in the hatch, rush in and club him with this."

Johnson backed off, holding up empty hands. "No way, man. I couldn't hit someone with that. My, God, you could kill a man if you hit him with that!"

Digger straightened and turned. "What's that? You there, Bishop? Goddamn it, don't be fucking with me when I'm drunk." He stared into the dark, blinking in the pelting rain for a minute. He spotted Zolotow's white lab coat. "That you, Dr. Alahandro? You better get in out of this rain." Then he turned back to the Bronco. "Ain't nobody around here got any common sense," he growled. He found the right key, bent over, and thrust it at the lock, missing the keyhole. "Shit." He took another stab at it, missed again.

"Do it!" Zolotow hissed at Johnson.

Johnson shook his head emphatically from side to side, raindrops slinging from his hair. He looked a lot like Razor when he did this.

"Gotcha!" Digger bellowed and all three of them froze. But he was only talking about the lock on the Bronco. The hatch went up with a wet hiss.

Zolotow shook Johnson by the shoulder. "Damn it, man, I'm injured and I can't move fast enough. If he's armed —"

"I can't," Johnson whined.

"What the fuck's in this damn thing anyway?" Digger muttered. A knife flashed silver in the rain and he began cutting at the duct tape, his lanky frame hunched over beneath the dripping hatch of the Bronco.

"You have to!"

"I'm a scientist," Johnson pleaded. "I ain't no fucking Chuck Norris!"

Digger sliced through the last of the tape and unsnapped the lid on the Igloo.

"Shit." Zolotow pushed Johnson away and started around the truck.

Kendra pushed past him. "Whoever said that men were the stronger sex was full of shit," she ranted. Zolotow tried to grab her, but she was wet and slippery. "Goddamn bunch of pansy ass, whiney baby, teat sucking…"

Whatever else she had to say was cut off as Digger caught her movement out of the corner of his eye. He turned and leered at her breasts bouncing beneath the damped cotton halter. "Oh, baby, am I glad to see you," he said, but then he registered the two men behind her and the fact that the one in the coat was definitely not Alahandro. "What the fuck's going on?" he growled, brandishing the knife.

"Nothing," Kendra replied sweetly, just before she kicked the knife from his hand. Digger's mouth dropped open in astonishment. It was only open a second, though, before Kendra's spinning hook kick closed it. "Kyai!" she screamed, her little five four frame a good eighteen inches off the ground in order for her foot to connect with Digger's jaw. Digger stumbled back against the Bronco's rear bumper, smacking the back of his head on the hatch, blood erupting from his nose and mouth. Kendra followed through with the ridge of her hand to his Adam's apple. He gagged and reached up for his neck. She brought a knee up into his groin. When this doubled the tall man over, she brought both hands down across the back of his head. He dropped face first into the mud and didn't move.

"Holy shit," said Johnson.

Razor rushed over and sniffed at Digger, then cocked his head at Kendra and gave her a look that mirrored Daryl Johnson's.

Zolotow reappraised the woman. That she'd recognized the Blake quote told him she was very educated — not run-off-at-the-mouth educated like Johnson, but certainly literate as hell. Now he'd just discovered that she had a black belt. He wondered how much more he'd learn about her if he was only given the time.

They searched the unconscious man, but he wasn't carrying a gun. The knife was lost in the dark and the mud somewhere. They left him there with the toes of his cowboy boots buried in the mud. Zolotow took the keys from the hatch and slammed it closed. Then he gave Kendra a quick hug. "Remind me not to piss you off," he said. "I wish I'd had you along when Earl started practicing his homers." Johnson stood well back, his previous affection for her lost in the scuffle. He looked as if he realized he'd been taking his life in his own hands when he'd been fondling the tender velvet of her bare shoulders.

"I had four brothers who were all gang members," Kendra explained. "They taught me not to be just another gang-bang girl." She looked away and added, bitterly, "It didn't keep me off the streets, but it did show me how to make sure I always got paid. Between that and the junior college I was going to, I stayed a very busy girl." She cast a glance at Daryl Johnson. "Never really had time for proper dating."

Zolotow squeezed her arm. "Let's trade family histories later, hon. Right now, Johnson and I need to be going."

She looked up at him, her eyes suddenly cold in the darkness. "You and Johnson?"

"I need you to get your lady friends ready to move." He leaned close and met her gaze. "I'll be back for you. Thirty minutes, tops. I'm just going down the road to the nearest telephone. Once that call is made, I'm coming back for you and the other girls."

She blinked in the rain, her lips tightly set.

"I promised to get you out of here, didn't I? I told you it was over."

"Take me with you," she said. "You said you'd take me with you."

"I want to get all the girls out of here, Kendra. I need you to go wake them up, get them ready to move. I'll be right back.

I promise. I won't leave you. And there's one other thing; I need you to create a diversion. Someone in the house is going to come looking for this moron. Or someone will hear me start this Bronco. Any way you look at it, we're going to get more attention than we need when we go to leave here. How are your matches?"

She pulled them from the pocket of her shorts. The matches, like everything else on her, were soaked through and through.

"You can probably find more in the barn. I want you to set it on fire. Light the straw in several places and the rest will take care of itself. While the barn's burning, you get the other girls ready to go. When I come back, everyone will be fighting the fire. We'll be driving the Bronco and his rental car." He snapped at Johnson, "What kind of car is it?"

"Uh ... it's blue. A Chevy something or other. I "

"Never mind. It'll be with this Bronco," he told Kendra. "We'll cut across that field there, back behind the barn, and we'll get as close to those buildings as possible." He pointed toward where he guessed the women were being held. "That's right, isn't it? That's where they are?"

Kendra merely nodded. She looked beaten, and for the first time she was shivering in the rain. She thought he wasn't coming back. He saw it in her eyes.

"I'll be back for you, Kendra. Be ready. It'll be a tight squeeze getting all the girls into the vehicles, but we'll manage. Understand? I *will* be back for you."

She nodded again.

"Good girl. You get that fire going." He kissed her cheek and pushed her toward the barn. "Stay with her, Razor." The rottweiler growled at him.

He unlocked the Bronco and was about to get in when he saw the gear shift and the clutch. He hadn't realized the Bronco had a standard transmission. He'd been, at best, only semi-conscious while Coop had chauffeured him around. He'd planned to drive with his left leg, because he couldn't bend the right one, but there was no way he could work the clutch and the throttle with only his left leg. "Johnson, you're driving." He tossed the grad student the keys. "Hurry."

They watched to make sure Kendra reached the barn safely. When she disappeared inside, Johnson started the engine and shifted into first gear. The truck lurched and stalled. "Easy," Zolotow told him, wondering if the kid knew how to drive a standard transmission. Johnson started the Bronco again and, with a series of neck-jarring lurches, got them moving.

They'd only gone forty feet when floodlights all across the front of the house came on, lighting the entire front yard clean out to the main road over a hundred feet away.

"Floor it!" Zolotow yelled. The tires spun in the mud and the vehicle slewed sideways until Johnson got it under control.

A gun barked and the rear window exploded. Several more gunshots followed.

The Bronco careened out onto the wet pavement and spun around until they were staring into the blinding lights from the house. Then, it stalled. Cursing, Johnson stomped the clutch and turned the key. As the engine growled back to life, the windshield exploded. The rearview mirror simply disappeared. Another bullet *spanged* off the corner of the hood.

Zolotow slammed the dash with the pipe wrench. "If you don't get us out of here, Johnson, I'm going to use this wrench on you!"

Johnson swung the Bronco around in a tire-squealing turn that dropped their left front tire into the roadside ditch. Zolotow feared for a moment that they'd get stuck, but the Bronco plowed through, bouncing Zolotow so hard that his head smacked the roof. He reached back and pulled the seatbelt around him. "Drive like you just got caught with the farmer's daughter!"

Johnson worked his way clumsily through the gears, jerking the vehicle this way and that as if the steering wheel and the shift lever were somehow connected, but at least he didn't stall the Bronco again. At seventy, he eased back on the throttle. The wipers were having a difficult time clearing the rain from the jagged remains of the windshield. It was nearly impossible to see. Headlights spun wildly behind them and then, a moment later, targeted their rear bumper.

Zolotow smacked Johnson in the shoulder and pointed through the hole in the fractured glass. "See that center line right in front of you. Watch that and floor this bitch!" He turned in his seat and looked back, hoping to see the first flames of the fire Kendra was to set, but the headlights behind them blinded him to everything beyond. There were two sets of headlights, both fairly high off the ground. Pick up trucks. He wished, belatedly, that they'd been able to find Digger's knife and use it on the tires of the other vehicles.

"You think," Johnson asked hesitantly, "that when all this is over, Kendra would maybe go out on a date with me?"

Zolotow just stared at him. "You're asking me if you should ask her out on a date?"

"Yeah."

"Do you have any fucking idea what kind of day I'm having?"

The two trucks came on fast, their headlights casting eerie water sprites in the spray coming off the Bronco.

"I'm just saying ... I mean ... do you think a guy like me would stand much of a chance with a girl like her?"

Obviously Daryl Johnson was completely unaware of just what Kendra did for a living. She'd all but out and out said it there in the rain, standing beside the Bronco after kicking Digger's ass, but Johnson must have been daydreaming about what lay beneath that wet halter top.

"The worst fucking day of my life," Zolotow said, "and you want me to give you romantic advice? Now I've heard everything."

"Well, you could be having a worse day," Johnson replied, ambivalent to the headlights that had now lit up the interior of the Bronco. "I saw something in the paper not too long ago, about these fire fighters in California. They had just put out this big forest fire and, in the middle of the burn, they found this dead guy. Only, strangest thing, the dead guy is wearing scuba gear. Wetsuit. Face mask. Tanks. The whole nine yards."

I think I saw that article, Zolotow started to say, but his mind was suddenly elsewhere. There was something else he'd read in the paper just the other day. Something his mind was trying to cough up, but it wouldn't quite come. It had something to do with the mysterious Beauchamps.

"And if that ain't strange enough, finding this scuba diver, dead in the middle of a forest fire, the autopsy showed that he had died, not from burns or even smoke inhalation, but from massive internal injuries. Well, anyway, they identified the poor son of a bitch from his dental records. Turns out the guy had been out scuba diving that day, twenty some miles from the fire. These big helicopters with water buckets had managed to scoop him up with a load of water for putting out the fire. Then they dropped the poor guy from several hundred feet. Let me tell you, Martin, that guy was having a bad day!"

In a flash of lightning, Zolotow saw someone — Bishop perhaps — leaning from the passenger window of the nearest truck, aiming a shotgun. Long, unkempt hair peeled back by the wind. Eyes squinted against the onslaught of wind and rain. A second later the gun belched fire. The rear of the Bronco sounded as if it had been hit with a handful of ball bearings.

"They're gaining on you!"

Johnson looked up for the rearview mirror, cursed when he saw it was gone. "I can't see!" he moaned, meaning the road in front of them. It was an old, back road and no one had thought to repaint the stripes in the last decade or so. If a sudden curve came up with no warning, they were dead.

The nearest truck rear-ended them. The Bronco lurched, its front end doing a little hop that sent them careening from one side of the road to the other. Johnson nearly lost control. The headlights on the truck behind them shattered and went out. Somehow, over the road noise and the pounding rain, Zolotow thought he heard glass tinkling on the highway. The passenger in the truck, his face a baleful red in the Bronco's tail lights, raised the shotgun and fired again. The cooler and the rear seat caught most of the blast, but pellets riddled the interior. Johnson cursed and grabbed at a bloody ear. Zolotow felt new pain in his shoulder and the back of his neck.

"This is pissing me off!" Johnson yelled and slammed on the brakes.

Zolotow was thrown against his seatbelt, wrenching his back and side. The truck slammed into the back of the Bronco with a thundering crash. Zolotow saw the driver smack his face into the windshield hard enough to crack the glass. The passenger lost the shotgun out the window. The weapon tumbled end-over-end, bouncing off the road and out into the prairie somewhere.

Johnson floored the Bronco again with a laugh that sounded maniacal. "Teach those boys to mess with me. I got a lady friend to ask out to dinner." He reached out and punched off the headlights.

"What the hell are you doing?"

"Watch."

Johnson slowed down and allowed the truck to pull up on Zolotow's side. Ahead of them lay nothing but a black void and rain, impenetrable with both sets of vehicle lights out. The truck's passenger was now armed with a handgun. Reaching across the driver, he took aim on Zolotow.

"Shit!" Zolotow yelled.

"Not to worry," replied Johnson and suddenly he swerved the Bronco over to slam into the side of the pickup. The man with the handgun was thrown against his door. The firearm was flung from his hand. The driver struggled to maintain control of his vehicle as it careened wildly across the road and onto the shoulder.

And then Zolotow saw what Johnson had done. It rushed at them like a brick wall out of the dark and the rain. One minute there was nothing but empty road ahead and the next there was instant death, invisible because Johnson had killed the headlights. The rental car. He'd left the rental car on the side of the road. The truck hit it at nearly eighty miles an hour and erupted in a great ball of flame. The impact was deafening. Metal and glass and bright tongues of flame hung with the Bronco for a moment, and then they were past it, with nothing but a tire rolling alongside them where the truck had been. The tire lost momentum, veered off the side of the road, and disappeared into the dark prairie. The Bronco topped a rise, leaving the ground for a moment. When Zolotow looked back, there was nothing but an orange sheen to the falling rain back beyond the rise.

And then ... the second set of headlights, gaining on them.

"Oh, God," moaned Johnson, as he reached down and switched the headlights back on. "I killed those men, didn't I?"

"They would have surely killed us," Zolotow told him.

"But ... Oh, God. Oh, God. I killed them. I didn't think it through. I just acted. I killed them."

Zolotow gripped his arm. "Get a hold of yourself. The second truck is coming. I don't need you cracking up on me now."

"They're dead. I killed them."

An automatic weapon opened up from behind. Bullets did a tap dance across the back end of the Bronco, thunked into the cooler, hissed through the rear seat. One slipped between the two men and shattered the AM-FM cassette. Another punched through the back of Zolotow's seat, grazed both his arm and his injured side, and popped open the glove compartment. *By mere inches are we saved*, thought Zolotow. It's wasn't the first time for him.

"Faster!"

"I can't see!"

The road took a curve to the left and Johnson nearly lost control. For one sickening second, Zolotow felt the rear end slip; then the tires grabbed, and the Bronco shuddered through the turn. A sign flashed by and Zolotow just had time to make it out.

"Another curve coming up," he warned.

"I saw it."

"Kill the lights again."

"Are you crazy?"

"Kill them! And whatever happens, don't you dare touch your foot to the brakes."

Johnson reached down and hit the lights. Their world collapsed in darkness again. He took his foot off the throttle as they went into the curve, leaning forward until his face nearly filled

the hole in the spider-webbed windshield. Blinking in the blinding rain, he tried to hug the center line, but he lost it and the left hand tires were suddenly churning up mud. He fought to keep the vehicle on the road. At that speed, the tires hung up on the edge of the asphalt, groaning like pit bulls with their jaws locked on an enemy. The Bronco tipped. For a horrifying span of time in which his heart quit beating, Zolotow thought they were going over. He had time to notice that Johnson had never buckled his own seatbelt. Then the vehicle righted itself, lurched several feet to the right, and acquired the road, fish-tailing madly until Johnson fought it under control in the straight away beyond the curve. Never once had he
touched the brake pedal.

    Zolotow turned to look back. The pickup driver missed the warning sign. He'd been focused on the Bronco, more than likely confused when it suddenly vanished into the darkness. Without the Bronco's taillights to navigate by, he didn't see the turn until it was too late. Zolotow watched as the truck spun off the road and tumbled end over end. Their headlights died before the vehicle stopped rolling, and he lost it in the darkness. No flames. No explosion. But no one could have walked away from a crash like that.

    "Slow down, we've lost them."

    Johnson was shaking like a leaf.

    "I said we lost them. Turn the lights back on."

    "Okay. I…"

    And then something darted out in front of them.

    Johnson yelped and jerked the wheel hard to the left. Zolotow didn't know what the grad student thought he'd seen. There was no time to ask. The Bronco sluiced sideways through a deep patch of water on the road. The tires left the ground. And then they were rolling.

    Glass was suddenly everywhere. The roof came down and smacked Zolotow on the top of his head. The Igloo slammed into the back of his seat and burst open. The pipe wrench went through what was left of the windshield. Johnson was there one minute and then he was gone, one of his shoes whistling past

Zolotow's nose.

Noise.

Pain.

The smell of gasoline and the terror of flames.

And the smell of something else, too. Coppery. Brine-like. Red.

The passenger door jabbed him in the side and the dash folded down on his legs. Gravity couldn't decide how it should be oriented. He heard someone scream and realized it was himself.

Then everything came to a bone-jarring halt and he lay there trying to breathe. "A tumbleweed," he moaned. "It was a goddamn tumbleweed." He tried to laugh, but he was too busy shaking. The silence in the aftermath of the wreck was baffling. It was as if the world had stopped breathing. There was nothing but the rain and the ticking of the Bronco's engine.

And then Zolotow noticed the blood. It was everywhere. He was coated with it. It ran from the interior of the vehicle, pooling with the rain in his lap. His white lab coat had gone red. He checked himself over, thinking to have lost so much blood so quickly he had to have opened a jugular or a femoral artery. But he was okay. It wasn't his blood.

"Johnson?" he moaned.

And then his questing hands found something in the crumbled, dark interior of the Bronco. It was an arm. A human arm. Severed midway between the shoulder and the elbow. It was the arm of a young black man.

"Johnson!" Zolotow yelled.

He imagined the young man lying somewhere in the mud, unconscious, his arm ripped off and blood spewing from the ragged stump. Zolotow had to hurry if he was going to reach him in time to save his life. Scrambling, he worked his legs free of the twisted dash, ignoring his own pain. He was halfway through the gaping windshield, the Bronco's hood warm beneath his arms, the collapsed roof tearing the lab coat, when several things came crashing in on him. It was as if he'd been stumbling along with his eyes closed, and he'd suddenly decided to open them to a blinding light.

The blood in the vehicle was cold. Icy cold. There were vaporous tendrils emanating wherever it encountered the warm rain.

The arm was cold, too. And the arm wasn't bleeding.

There were broken plastic bags littered throughout the bloody interior of the Bronco. The Igloo was in the back seat, where it had ended up after slamming into Zolotow's headrest. There were more bags inside, bloated red and unbroken, packed in smoking dry ice. In the back of his mind, Zolotow heard Coop telling McDevitt: *You were absolutely right. There ain't nothing that ain't for sale in California.* And what else would vampires fly to California to buy, besides a little of the west coast's finest vintage?

And the newspaper. Why had it taken him so damn long to remember what he'd read in the newspaper? He'd seen the article in the *LA Times* about the diver scooped up and dumped on a forest fire. One minute the poor bastard had been breast stroking in the Pacific Ocean, and the next he'd been falling into a blazing inferno. Now, finally, he remembered another article, too.

Beauchamps.

An out-of-stater by that name had been murdered in L.A. just the day before Zolotow took Debbie to the airport. Zolotow had read it in that morning's paper, seated at the table trying not to watch Debbie picking at the eggs he'd fixed her, trying not to think about saying goodbye to her, hoping for something in the paper that would take his mind off the hollow place in his chest. Beauchamp's body had been found, minus an arm, in a less-than-reputable hotel when he'd failed to check out at noon. LAPD had no suspects. It was unknown what had become of the arm. The authorities were making arrangements to have the body sent home to... Where else? Oklahoma.

He slid from the hood of the Bronco and collapsed in the mud. The stir sticks taped to his knee had broken in the crash. The duct tape still provided some support, but not enough for him to stand in his present condition. He half crawled, half crab-walked away from the vehicle.

"Johnson!"

"Here," came a weak voice out of the wet gloom.

Zolotow found him not more than thirty feet away, tangled in sage grass and a barbed-wire fence.

"Did I hit it?"

"What? Hit what?" Zolotow almost screamed at him. "You were dodging tumbleweeds, son!"

"No, it was a dog. I saw it."

"Bullshit. Lie still. Your leg's broken. You should wear your damn seat belt, you know?" Zolotow ran his hands down the twisted limb, feeling the shattered, misaligned bones, but finding no breaks in the skin, no blood other than what was oozing from barbed-wire cuts. Johnson was very lucky.

"Don't try to tell me what I saw," Johnson argued. "I saw a dog. He ran right across the road in front of me."

"Well, then, it was a tumbleweed shaped like a dog. Your panhandle Okies have taken up tumbleweed topiary. I hear it's all the rage."

"I'm telling you, it was a dog! She would never go out with me if I killed a dog, would she?"

Zolotow tried to work the twisted leg free of the barbed wire, but Johnson cried out in pain. "Sorry."

"It's okay. I'm okay. Shit. Hurts like hell. She'll go out with me if I ask her, won't she, Zolotow? I mean, I'm not real good at this. I guess I'm something of a nerd. Spend more time in the lab with cultures than I do with women. Computers I know. DNA sequences I know. Woman are a mystery."

"Hell, that's what makes them fun, son."

"But will she go out with me?"

"Yeah, she'll go out with you." Zolotow decided there and then that he'd pay the bill if he had to. The kid would get his date. He'd never even have to know Kendra was ... Shit, what word would even get through to the kid? Prostitute? Whore? Painted Lady? Harlot? Trollop? No matter. Zolotow wasn't going to burst his bubble. "Now be still, I've got to try and get some help. I can't get you out of this damn fence. We —"

At that moment headlights washed over them, accentuated with the blue and red strobes of a police car.

Zolotow let out a sigh. "We're okay, Daryl. The cavalry's here." He raised himself up out of the mud and the desert sage and waved at the patrol car as it pulled off the side of the road. "Here!" he yelled. "We're over here. We need help."

It was a county sheriff. He approached them with his gun drawn. Blue uniform with stripes down the outside of his trouser legs. There was a ridiculous looking plastic bag keeping his hat dry.

"We're unarmed," Zolotow told him. "My friend needs help."

"Sit tight," said the sheriff.

"Not a problem, officer. Neither of us is going anywhere."

The sheriff unclipped a cell phone from his belt, flipped it open and dialed a number.

"We're safe now, right, Zolotow?" Johnson asked. His lips were blue and trembling. His eyes had that nervous, trapped animal look to them.

Zolotow squinted through the rain and watched as the county sheriff listened to the phone ring. "No," he said softly. "I think we're fucked." County sheriffs don't call in highway accidents on cell phones. They use their radio.

The phone quit ringing. "Yeah, it's me ... I've got them. About four miles south. No, I haven't checked yet, but I'd say your boys are dead or messed up pretty bad. Both your trucks are off the road somewhere."

"Tell him a couple of those boys are crispy critters," Zolotow said. "Tell him we're real sorry about Coop's Bronco, but there was a tumbleweed looked just like a dog. Tell him to get us an ambulance or I'll —"

The sheriff pointed his service revolver at Zolotow's head. "Shut the fuck up."

"Standard Okie greeting," Zolotow remarked to Johnson. "They don't mean anything by it."

"Yeah," said the sheriff into the phone, "I'll sit with them till you get here, then we need to figure out how to explain all this. Needs to be quick, before I wind up with local residents to deal with." The sheriff closed the cell phone and clipped it back to his belt. "Ya'll just sit tight." He grinned. "Help's on the way."

Zolotow leaned into Johnson, trying to take some of the young man's weight off the broken leg tangled in the barbed wire. "You're going to be okay," he whispered.

Another set of headlights appeared to the south. It was the wrong direction for McDevitt and company. The headlights slowed down and pulled to the side of the road behind the patrol car.

"Shit." The cop holstered his revolver. "One word out of either of you and you're going to wish your daddies had pulled out early." He tromped back through the mud toward the road.

The doors on the other vehicle — it looked like a pickup, but Zolotow was having trouble seeing through the rain and the lights — opened, and two men got out. "Do you need help, officer?" called one of the newcomers. Zolotow thought the voice sounded familiar. As the two men walked around their truck and approached the sheriff, Zolotow thought he recognized the bow-legged swagger, the boots, the hats. Both men were wearing ankle-length rain slickers, beneath which damn near anything could be concealed. Zolotow opened his mouth to say something; then decided it didn't really matter one way or the other.

The sheriff waved them back. "Thanks, but there's just been a bit of an accident here. A couple drunks went off the road in the rain. I've got it under control."

One of the approaching men suddenly raised a shotgun he'd concealed under his slicker. The 12 gauge boomed and most of the sheriff's head disappeared. He fell without making a single cry, splashing into the mud where his legs twitched for a few minutes, and then he was still. The man with the shotgun paused, looked down at the sheriff's brains oozing into the mud, chuckled softly, then stepped over him and splashed through the mud toward Zolotow and Johnson. The rain running down the gunman's face detoured around the scars on his cheek.

"Howdy, Earl," said Zolotow. "And is that Bert or Ernie with you? I never could tell the difference. You leave Billy Ray at home?"

"Still got a mouth, doncha?" Earl nudged Johnson with the shotgun. "Who's this?"

"Kid works for me," Zolotow lied. "Does research. Runs down facts. Occasionally he brings me stuff. You know, gopher work."

Earl frowned in the rain and stroked his shotgun. "You sure he don't work for McDevitt?"

"Would I be making my getaway with one of McDevitt's thugs in tow?"

"Reckon not. You were supposed to be making your getaway with Toby's daughter though."

"Now, Earl, I had the impression you really didn't care whether I came back with her or not."

"Yeah? What gave you that idea?"

"Could have been the sendoff I got."

Earl tipped back his hat and smiled. "Was a hell of an ass-kicking, wasn't it?"

The big black man, Bert or Ernie, one of the Uzi brothers, stepped forward. "What's this about an ass-kicking? Toby said—"

Earl turned and shot the big man in the gut. For a moment, he stood there, blood and guts darkening his shredded slicker, viscera trailing down the legs of his jeans and over the toes of his boots. His white eyes were wide and bright in the night. A gust of wind took the hat from his head and sent it off across the prairie in search of tumbleweeds shaped like dogs. Then his knees buckled and he just crumpled in place, folding in on himself and splashing into the mud, a much smaller man than he had been one shotgun blast ago. Earl raised the shotgun to his shoulder, sighted, and blew the man's head off.

Zolotow said nothing.

Johnson said nothing.

The rain continued to fall across a prairie that was eerily silent.

"Just his rotten luck," Earl said. "Toby got to thinking about racial segregation and how his employees ought to get to know one another better. You know, white men and niggers, all getting along together like we was brothers or something. Billy Ray has to hang out with Bubba, and poor old Ernie got stuck with me. Bad timing. Just plain old bad timing." He kicked Zolotow out of the way and raised the shotgun, taking aim on Johnson. "No big deal though. Only good nigger's a dead nigger, far as I'm concerned."

Johnson whimpered. Zolotow struggled to his knees, about to lunge at the gunman.

Headlights came around the bend where the second truck had gone off the road earlier. Earl turned and looked back over his shoulder. "Whoops. Reprieve for you, boy." He lowered the shotgun and hid it under his slicker. "Company coming."

It was the Mercedes. When Earl saw who it was, he relaxed, no longer concerned about concealing the shotgun.

McDevitt walked from the road, wearing a khaki London Fog raincoat over his coveralls. The rain glistened off the bald dome of his head. One of his henchmen — maybe it was Digger, cause it was a tall SOB — waited by the Mercedes, looking miserable in the rain without a coat. McDevitt paused by the dead sheriff. "Goddamn it, Earl! This old boy was on my payroll!"

Earl shrugged sheepishly. "Sorry, Jimmy. He didn't say nothing 'bout it to me."

McDevitt continued to the next body, Ernie's.

"One of Toby's boys," Earl explained without being asked. "Toby sent us both out to see what was up with Coop and Zolo. Asshole kept farting in the truck, ever since he ate that Big Mac outside of Woodward. I'd had just about enough of that."

McDevitt stepped over Ernie's body without even looking at it and stopped before Zolotow and Johnson. "Who the hell is this?" he asked, pointing to Johnson.

"Zolo said it was some assistant of his," Earl replied, "but the asshole's probably lying. Sumbitch never tells the truth 'bout nothing."

"Seems like the thing to do while in Oklahoma," Zolotow said softly. "Lying and betrayal seem to be everyone's favorite past time."

Earl kicked his bad knee. "Shut up." He looked to McDevitt. "I was just about to kill 'em both." He raised the shotgun. "You want me to get on with it?"

"Check that one for a wallet," said McDevitt. "I want to know who he is."

Earl knelt and rolled Johnson over to get at his hip pocket. Johnson screamed as his broken leg was twisted. Earl held up the injured man's wallet and tried to read a driver's license in the gloom. "Johnson. Daryl Johnson. OKC address."

McDevitt thought for a minute. Then, "Yeah, okay, I know who he is."

Earl glanced at Johnson's credit cards, smiling mischievously, then slipped the wallet into a pocket. "Want I should plug him?"

"No. Go stand over by your truck."

"Huh?"

"I said, go stand over by your truck, Earl."

Earl looked confused, but he left.

McDevitt knelt beside Johnson. However, he was looking at Zolotow. "Confused?"

"Considerably."

"Earl works for me."

"I figured that one out."

McDevitt nodded. His eyes were blue-white, like Coop's. The rain ran from his pasty face like it was the hood of just-waxed show car. "Toby called and told me you were sent to kill me. That was a lie."

"Been a lot of things in my time," Zolotow acknowledged, "but an assassin is not one of them."

"Earl called a couple hours ago, first chance that he'd had to do so, and set things straight. Told me Toby sent you to rescue his daughter. I guess after you left, Toby changed his mind, figured it might be easier to sell you out and get his daughter back that way. I'd actually been thinking about letting you go come morning." Yeah, Zolotow believed that. "Course, I thought you were safely tucked away in my barn. A barn, I might add, which is presently burning to the ground. I don't suppose you had anything to do with that."

"Never been an arsonist either," Zolotow replied.

"Uh huh. Anyway, I can't let you go now." He glanced at the two bodies stretched out in the mud. "Gone way beyond that good old point of no return. I've got to figure out what to do with you."

"Don't forget Coop's part in all this. I'd like to see him get some kind of reward for all his efforts."

"Don't worry, I've a good use for Brother Cooper. I'm going to let you live just a wee bit longer so you can see how that works out."

"Does it involve Beauchamps' arm?"

The rain began to back off. The clouds parted and the moon tried to peek through. McDevitt's eyes, however, gleamed of their own light. "You're not such a bad detective after all, Zolotow! Too bad Toby got cold feet and sold you out. You might have actually brought his precious daughter home to him."

"I'd be happy to settle for a plane ticket home. You can all go about the business of killing each other off without me."

"Bet you would. Too late for that now. You're going to take part in our coon hunt tomorrow. I think you'll find it very stimulating. As for this young buck..." McDevitt turned and studied Johnson. "...I've only one use for him." He smiled, and an errant moonbeam caught his filed teeth, flashing opalescent and wet.

Zolotow launched himself at the big man, wishing he'd hung on to the pipe wrench. McDevitt turned his weak blows aside easily enough, twisting Zolotow's arm in a lock that pulled the damaged ribs in his side. Next thing Zolotow knew he was lifted high and then slammed to the ground, like a professional wrestler, only a professional wrestler has a ring to land on, with shock absorbers and a mat and a proper rehearsal beforehand. Zolotow lay there and tried to breathe, while McDevitt grabbed Johnson by the hair and jerked his head back to expose his throat.

Johnson screamed as his leg was pulled taut against the barbed wire restraining it. Zolotow tried to get up, but his body had quit on him. His mind flashed on another night and an alley in San Antonio. He'd laid there then, hurt and unable to move, while a beautiful, young prostitute's throat was cut. He hadn't been able to get up and save her.

Somehow he sucked in a great gasp of air and heaved himself up to a sitting position. McDevitt's ghost eyes tracked him with something akin to admiration as he lurched to his feet and stumbled forward. As McDevitt's jaws closed down and silenced Johnson's scream to a gurgling moan of terror, Zolotow hurled himself at the man again, pummeling the broad back beneath the rain coat. McDevitt pushed him back. Scrambling in the mud, Zolotow heard the crunch of cartilage as McDevitt ripped out Johnson's throat. He doubled his fists together and brought them down with all his might across the back of the bastard's bald head.

McDevitt turned and kicked Zolotow's bad knee out from under him. Zolotow went down in the mud. For a moment, McDevitt stood over him, Johnson's blood running from his mouth and down his chin, trailing in crimson striations across the pale marble of his chest to disappear under the coveralls. Zolotow tried to get back up and McDevitt kicked him in the face. Zolotow went down in the mud, his head reeling and the strength gone from every limb, while McDevitt returned to Johnson's ravaged throat, plunged his mouth into the glistening, pumping red hole there, and drank deeply.

The rain stopped and the moon looked down on the bloody prairie. The only sounds were Zolotow's incoherent rage and McDevitt's feeding.

Interlude: "I'd like to talk about your memory problem."

Zolotow stared at her blankly.

Dr. Mary Ellis formed a tent with her hands, her elbows on the desktop, and leaned her chin on the tips of her fingers. Silently they stared at each other. "Well?" she asked.

"I'm sorry," he said, "what was the question?" His joke fell flat. A nervous leg belayed his humor. When he saw her take note of it, he forced the leg to be still. "Mixed cerebral dominance," he finally said, nodding toward the folders stacked on her desk, "I'm sure it's all there in your files."

"I want to hear what it means to you."

He shrugged. "It means I forget things sometimes. Trivial things," he lied. "Nothing important. Last names. Phone numbers. Email addresses. Insignificant things like that. I take a lot of notes. I refer to them when I need to."

"Have the doctors ever identified the cause of this ... dysfunction?"

Zolotow didn't like the way she said that word. And he sure didn't like her prying into his past. Where he'd been, who he'd known, what he'd done before he joined the police force, was his business. As far as the department knew, he came from a long line of foster homes. He would not allow some over-educated head doctor to lay the blame for what he was on his dead parents.

"I've been told," he said, giving her nothing that she wouldn't already know, "that MCD is much like dyslexia, which they now believe results from serious damage to the left cerebral hemisphere. The injury results in the brain never establishing a definitive right or left dominance." He held up his hands. "Look, Ma, ambidextrous."

She nodded. "I'm familiar with the theory. But the injury has to occur just after brain lateralization, between the ages of, say, six to eight years old. I checked through all your medical records. There's nothing about a childhood injury of this type."

He knew that was only because his records didn't go back that far. He stared at her, daring her to probe further. Silence reigned for several minutes.

"Okay," she said, breaking the tableau. "So you don't recall an injury that might have caused this. And, of course, the theories don't necessarily apply, since you don't have dyslexia. You exhibit none of the normal reading or cognitive disorders associated with that disorder." She arched an eyebrow. "Right?"

"When I was young, I had some reading problems. Fierce headaches. Difficulty remembering what I had read. Occasional problems with comprehension. I overcame the problems by wearing tinted lenses and teaching myself to memorize what I read."

She brightened. "That explains the poetry!"

"Yeah. I memorized poetry, tons of it. Yeats, Dickinson, Tennyson... everything I could get my hands on. It was like my memory was a jumbled toolbox. Memorizing the poetry established order in that chaos, forced a structure where none had been before. It arranged the toolbox so that I could find things, so I could store other things in a place where I could find them later."

"But you still forget some things?"

"Occasionally." He knew if he wanted to remain employed, he needed to steer her away from the subject of memory loss. How long before she realized there had been several cases where his memory loss had been a significant factor? True, he'd eventually solved those cases, but the local bureaucracy rarely took final results into account. Witch hunts had always possessed the power to galvanize otherwise complacent upper management into taking action.

He would have to offer her some other things, deficiencies which he could control, things that were already documented in his records.

"I suffer some of the standard side effects of MCD: poor spatial reasoning, right-left directional confusion, linear tracking errors, a failure to develop a "leading eye," occasional dizziness and poor balance. Televisions and computer monitors give me a mother of a headache."

"Yet they've allowed you to remain on the force?" she asked over her folded hands. She looked like she was praying now, perhaps asking for divine guidance on what to do with this totally unorthodox police detective, asking for the straw that would break the camel's back.

"My dysfunction, as you called it, has its benefits, too. I'm a wealth of trivia. Sometimes unrelated events just click together in my mind." He snapped his fingers. "I see connections that other detectives never do. You don't know how many times I've been handed cases on which everyone else failed to deliver." Well, maybe she did know; she had it all there in front of her in that six inch stack of file folders. He leaned forward in his chair, lowering his line of sight so their eyes lined up. "Check the records, lady. No one brings in the bad guys quite like I do."

FOUR: *Whorehouse Confessions and Lies — Bathtubs and Trollops — Rainbows and Phone Calls — Preparations and Guinea Pigs — Hunters and Prey*

The barn was a raging inferno when they returned to the hog farm. Great tongues of flame licked at the clouds. Sparks climbed up the sky on the falling rain which hissed and popped off the blackening timbers. The surrounding buildings writhed with reflected orange serpents. The side of the ranch house had become a giant living mural, shifting in the night like a theater screen, only the projector was broken, displaying everything in a color spectrum called fire. It looked as if McDevitt's men had tried to fight the fire at first, but had quickly given it up as a lost cause. They stood back from it now, shielding their faces with hats and bandannas, buckets slung useless from their hands. The only thing that kept the fire from spreading to the other buildings and the prairie was the rain. There were no fire trucks. Either McDevitt hadn't called for them or Beaver couldn't afford a fire department. In this downpour, odds were good that no one else would see either the flames or the column of smoke.

They dragged Zolotow past the burning barn and around to the buildings where he had arranged to rescue Kendra and her friends. Digger and another guy did the dragging, neither of them being gentle. Zolotow was beyond even attempting to walk. They hauled him along like a limp sack of potatoes. Digger, in particular, wasn't pleased about this. He kicked Zolotow several times, somehow managing to miss his ribs, back, and knee, proving that all Zolotow's luck wasn't used up.

The entire lower half of Digger's face was swollen and purple. Zolotow refrained from making any comment on this. For the moment, he was conserving his energy.

Earl had been left with instructions to round up the bodies — including those in McDevitt's pickup trucks — and bring them all back to the hog farm A.S.A.P. where Zolotow gathered that they would be disposed of by some nefarious means. Zolotow had heard somewhere that pigs will eat anything.

McDevitt himself had taken charge of Beauchamp's arm, tossing it into the trunk of the Mercedes (along with Zolotow). While Digger and the other considerate gentleman escorted Zolotow to the women's quarters, McDevitt took the arm and marched straight past the burning barn, around the house, and into the lab with it.

The door to the women's building featured a cipher lock, same as the ones on the lab. Digger punched in the code — the same code that Zolotow already knew from the lab. He didn't seem concerned that Zolotow saw it and, a moment later, Zolotow knew why.

"Jimmy said to change that number," Digger told the second guy. "Do it, while I make this sack of shit comfortable."

It occurred to Zolotow, somewhere in a small part of his brain that was still doggedly determined to figure everything out, that all they needed as proof that he'd been in the lab was the lab coat he was wearing. They might not know how he'd gotten the combination, but they knew he had it. They'd searched him, thinking he might have taken something, but all they'd found was Debbie's picture — which they'd kept. He had no way of knowing whether they knew about the email that he'd sent. He'd been careful to delete it from Garza's SENT folder, but that was no guarantee that their Internet server hadn't logged it as it went out.

Dragging him mostly by the hair, Digger escorted Zolotow inside. The door opened on a quaint little kitchen, complete with checkered curtains (which did not conceal the fact that there were bars on the window) and matching place mats on the table. Someone had done a mediocre job of applying flowered wallpaper. There were clean dishes stacked beside the sink. The clock display on the microwave oven blinked 2:48. It was hard to believe that just twenty-four hours ago he'd been lying in bed with Debbie in his arms, watching her sleep, memorizing the lines of her face and the way the sheets hugged her body.

Beyond the kitchen was a decent-sized living room. Carpet. Two large sofas and several armchairs in need of reupholstering. A stereo. A television set with rabbit ears. A coffee table several inches deep in *Cosmopolitan*, *People*, and *Reader's Digest*. The only light came from a table lamp with a natty shade. Despite its feeble glow, the water stains on the far wall and the ceiling were obvious. Someone had tried to hide the largest of the stains with a framed print of a thoroughbred racehorse. To the left was a bathroom, the door standing open, the seat and lid on the toilet in the proper *down* position. The shower curtain featured bright yellow daisies. Stacked on the rim of the tub were more bottles of shampoo and conditioner than a man could use in a lifetime. To the right was a long hallway down which there were closed doors as far as Zolotow's present vantage allowed him to see.

The whole place smelled like Chanel Number 5.

Digger dropped Zolotow face first to the floor. "Ladies!" he bellowed. "In the kitchen! Now!"

There came the sound of opening doors, followed by the patter of small, bare feet on the linoleum. Face to the floor, Zolotow was greeted by a bounty of dainty, painted toes and smooth, ebony ankles. He knew he was too far gone when he couldn't find the strength to follow the ankles up to the lovely legs and other treasures he knew were connected.

"Are any of the men in here?" Digger asked.

Several female voices assured him that all the men had left earlier when the fire was spotted.

"Good. No one is allowed in here tonight. No one is allowed in here until this piece of shit…" He kicked Zolotow again, sinking the sharp toe of his size 13 boot into Zolotow's gut. Zolotow tried to groan appropriately, but failed. He knew he was far gone when he could no longer voice his appreciation for the expert administration of pain. "…is gone. Understand? Anyone comes in here, you tell them Jimmy himself said that. The man who comes in here while this man is still here will be fed to the hogs. And so will the cunt who sleeps with him.

"Got it?"

They all assured him that they understood perfectly.

"Good. He won't be here long, but for the moment, with the barn burning to the ground, there ain't no other place to put him. Now, I want to know two things and if I don't find out real quick like, I'm gonna start knocking heads. I want to know which one of you is Toby Washington's daughter. And I want to know which one of you bushwhacked me an hour ago out in front of the house."

Silence.

Digger paced like a drill sergeant before his troops. Zolotow tried to look up, but his neck wouldn't track up the length of Digger's legs. Digger towered above him, impossibly tall. Unreachable.

"Okay, fine," Digger grumbled. "I'll leave figuring out the first answer to Jimmy, but I guarantee you whores ain't gonna like his methods of prying out the information. But I want to know right now which one of you it was that jumped me in the dark!"

When there was no response, he slapped one of them. The other girls barely reacted. Obviously, this was not a new scene for them. Abuse had become a part of their lives.

"Hey, Digger," Zolotow groaned. "Maybe when you figure out which one it was, you can take her place in here, being as how you're such a pussy."

"Shut up!" Digger kicked him in the head.

Zolotow spit blood out on the linoleum. It mingled colorfully with the rain and mud puddled around him. He was making a terrible mess on their nice clean floor. "Tell them how she damn near kicked your head off, Digger, how this little slip of a girl…"

Digger drew his leg back. "I said…"

"Digger." It was McDevitt's voice, from the doorway. "That's enough. You can go."

"I was just…"

"I said go."

"Sure, Jimmy."

McDevitt crossed the kitchen and knelt beside Zolotow. "How you holding up, cuz?"

"Got a terrible itch on my nose. You mind?"

"Your hands aren't tied."

"Oh."

"Way I slammed you, out there by the road, most men woulda up and died. You surprised me when you got up off the ground. You got some stones, Zolo."

Zolotow tried to smile, but he wasn't sure his facial muscles were responding properly. He tried to think of something clever to say, but nothing came to mind. He considered telling McDevitt the truth, that he planned to kill the albino son of a bitch as soon as the opportunity presented itself, but the whole thing seemed so melodramatic, like something in a bad Bruce Willis flick. Besides, he was afraid McDevitt would kick him. He'd had about all he could take. Come to think of it, he'd had about all he could take earlier in the day. It was one thing to stick his neck out to distract Digger from slapping around the women. It was another to taunt McDevitt.

"I'd ask you which one of these lovely ladies helped you out of the barn earlier, but you'd never tell me, would you?"

"I could tell you," Zolotow replied, "but then I'd have to kill you." That sounded terribly cliché, too. *I'm losing it*, Zolotow thought.

McDevitt sighed. "Sure, partner. I understand." He leaned close and whispered so only Zolotow could hear. "More'n one way to skin a cat, though. Know what I mean?" He got up and crossed to the kitchen counter. Zolotow heard a kitchen drawer open, followed by the rattle of silverware. The drawer closed and McDevitt returned to his side. Something sharp pricked the flesh just beneath Zolotow's right eye. Focusing on it made his head scream. It was a spoon, but it was a spoon with a serrated edge. It took Zolotow a minute to figure it out. Grapefruit spoon. Grapefruit would be just the kind of breakfast these nubile ladies would enjoy, what with having to watch their figures and all.

"Watch closely, ladies," said McDevitt. Zolotow could smell Johnson's blood on his breath. "Old Zolo's got some beautiful blue eyes, don't he? I bet you've had your share of women comment on those eyes, haven't you, cuz? I bet you've picked up more'n one bar fly on the strength of those baby blues." McDevitt poked him again with the spoon, drawing blood from Zolotow's lower eyelid. "Here's the deal, ladies. I know one of you helped this man earlier this evening. If I don't know who that someone was in the next ten seconds, I'm going to scoop out that beautiful baby blue eye of his."

"What makes you think they give a shit?" Zolotow asked, hoping Kendra would take the cue to keep her mouth shut.

McDevitt ignored him. "Ten ... nine..."

"It was me." Kendra's voice.

Zolotow sighed and tried to move.

McDevitt stood. "Good girl, Kendra. I think Zolo has suffered enough for one evening. I would have really hated to remove his eye. I have one other question for all of you. Who is Toby Washington's daughter?"

"That'd be me, too," Kendra lied. "Kendra Washington. That's why I helped him. I found him in the barn and he told me why he was here."

There was a moment of silence in which Zolotow imagined McDevitt drilling her with his ghost eyes, watching for some telltale sign that she was lying. Zolotow pictured Kendra meeting his stare, unblinking, her jet black eyes an intense dark mirror of McDevitt's own. The girl had spunk. She'd beat the shit outta Digger. She'd set that fire just like Zolotow had told her. She wasn't about to back down.

Finally, McDevitt tossed the spoon on the kitchen table. "Sleep well, ladies. We're having a hunt tomorrow evening. It'll be a special hunt. I'm going to let our good friend Zolo in on it. I expect, however, that he'll just slow you down." He turned and walked to the door. Just before he closed and locked it behind him, he called back over his shoulder, "You might want to think about that, Kendra, seeing as how you're definitely one of those we'll be hunting."

A half dozen pairs of soft hands rolled him over. Kendra took his head in her lap and wiped some of the mud and blood from his face. "Martin? Can you hear me?"

"Loud and clear. God, I hurt. Scratch my nose, would ya?"

"They changed the locks, Martin."

"I know."

"They're gonna kill us."

"We're not dead yet, darling." Famous last words.

"God, he stinks," said one of the girls.

"Sorry," Zolotow mumbled. "Cow manure."

"You were very brave, trying to keep Digger focused on you, so that he wouldn't hurt us."

"Ha. Stupid. Stupid's what I was."

"No," she whispered. "Brave." The other girls agreed with her.

"Yeah, well, bravery hurts like hell."

"We'll take care of you." Kendra starting barking orders at the other girls. "Taneesha, draw a hot bath. LaDonna, rip a couple bed sheets into long strips."

"Think maybe I could get something to eat, too?" Zolotow asked, weakly. "I haven't eaten anything since breakfast. Coop pissed off the stewardess, so I didn't even get any peanuts on the flight out here. We were about to eat some greasy burgers, but…"

"Shush, baby. Save your strength." She stroked his face. "We'll take care of you. You're in good hands now." Back over her shoulder: "Judy, could you cook some bacon and eggs, please?"

"Toast, too," Zolotow whispered. "And some coffee. Might check for some aspirin. Ibuprofen would be nice. Morphine, if you got it."

Kendra sent another of the girls (Tessa, the one in the pink t-back panties) to search their medicine cabinet. Another luscious female (Penny, whose long, sable legs should have been earning millions in pantyhose commercials instead of secreted away in Oklahoma) volunteered a joint she'd copped from one of the lab guys. Kendra had her light it, and then she held it to Zolotow's lips. "Smoke this."

"I could be charged with contributing to the delinquency of a minor."

"I'm twenty-one, Martin."

"Oh." He drew a deep breath of the marijuana and held it. "Legal age. That's good to know."

Someone called out that the tub was ready. Kendra had one of the girls help with Zolotow's pants. First, there was a struggle to remove all the duct tape. They stripped him naked, right there on the kitchen floor, tossing his clothes in the kitchen sink with half a bottle of detergent.

"Under other circumstances, this might be embarrassing," Zolotow mumbled. "I suppose it's okay, though, seeing as how you girls are all professionals."

"Quiet," Kendra told him. "Only about half these girls were taken off the streets. The rest came from good, middle-income homes. A couple are young mothers with children of their own at home."

"Oh. Mind helping me get my foot out of my mouth?"

"Don't worry about it," she told him, kissing his forehead. "You're mumbling so bad, I don't think any of them even heard you." Kendra pointed to an attractive girl who looked about sixteen. "This is Rayleen. Rayleen Washington."

Rayleen extended a hand. When Zolotow failed to take it, she placed it against his chest as if she were feeling for a heartbeat. "I'm sorry about all this, Mr. Zolotow." Her eyes were hazel. There were mulatto freckles on her cheeks. Her hair had copper highlights, as if she carried around her own sunlight. If she were any cuter, Zolotow thought, somebody'd be making Rayleen dolls and advertising them between Saturday morning cartoons. How the hell had Toby Washington produced this?

"Your daddy's worried about you, Rayleen."

"My daddy's a murdering son of a bitch, Mr. Zolotow. And if I get out of here alive, the last place you'll ever find me will be with him. I'm thinking I'd like to see California. Washington State maybe. Definitely Las Vegas."

Zolotow tried to smile at her. "I've kinda had my fill of

Oklahoma, too, Rayleen."

Six of them carried him to the bathtub and lowered him into the hot water. A couple bottles of good smelling oils and bubbly stuff got thrown in as well and, in short order, he was masked in a cloak of perfumed bubbles. He smoked Penny's pot and tried some old Zen tricks to compartmentalize his pain. One of the two was fairly effective. Zolotow's money was on the marijuana. Kendra and two of the other girls — Taneesha and LaDonna, he thought — stayed in the bathroom, scrubbing him down. Their silk teddy pajamas got splashed, but they didn't seem to mind. Soap bubbles climbed up their arms and dripped down their thighs, venturing into regions featured in many an adolescent dream. Watching them bend over to expose valleys of sweet milk chocolate between their breasts, feeling their hands on his body, smelling all the wonderful bathroom odors that accompany women, Zolotow regretted that he was too broken and battered and flat out exhausted to fully enjoy himself. He wondered if all his respective parts would ever be fully functional again.

LaDonna had her nails on his scalp and was working up a most luxurious shampoo lather, when Kendra finally asked the question Zolotow had been dreading. "What happened to Daryl Johnson?"

"Tumbleweed," Zolotow whispered. "Damn thing ran right out in front of us like it had a death wish or something." He looked away, finding it hard to meet her beautiful onyx eyes. "Johnson's ... dead."

She said nothing, but for a moment he thought she would cry. Maybe she'd actually become fond of the guy during their short acquaintance. Maybe she'd been holding out some hope that he'd escaped and might be returning any minute now with the cavalry. "Get him rinsed off," she told Taneesha and LaDonna. "Holler when you're done. Me and some of the others will come help you get him out of the tub."

"We putting him on the couch?" one of them asked. "I don't think he'll fit."

"No, we'll put him in my room."

They rinsed him off. Kendra and Tessa crowded into the

bathroom to help hold him up, so he could be dried. One of them was considerate enough to wrap a towel around his waist, and then they hauled him out, through the living room, and down the hallway. Kendra's room was the third door down. There was very little in the way of decoration, but the bed was a king size and the sheets were soft. The pillows smelled like Kendra. The mattress was comfortably broken in.

They wrapped his ribs and his knee in strips torn from a bed sheet. Taneesha demonstrated what she called her three months worth of experience at nursing school by picking shotgun pellets out of his neck and shoulder. She put a butterfly bandage on the cut over his eye. She explained that she stayed in practice applying bandages on her two boys at home. The boys were the reason she had quit nursing school in the first place. Then she got a faraway look in her eyes and went all quiet, while the other girls tried to find something that needed their attention. Taneesha's eyes welled up with tears and she excused herself.

He might have immediately fallen asleep, but Judy brought in a tray of food. She sat on the edge of the bed and hand fed him bacon and eggs, toast with strawberry preserves, and slices of orange. There was coffee and apple juice and half-naked women crowding into the room, watching his every move.

"I think these are the best eggs I've ever eaten," he told Judy.

"Cayenne pepper," she said, beaming, "that's the secret."

"Sorry," he said at one point. "I think I'm getting crumbs in the bed."

Judy kissed his cheek. "Don't worry about it, hon. Kendra complains, you can just move into my room. You can eat in my bed anytime you want."

He ate more than he would have thought possible. Told himself he needed to build up some strength. But he didn't want to seem rude either. When the food was gone, Kendra shooed the other girls out of the room, softly closed the door, and turned off the light.

The wind rattled the window pane behind the bed and moaned over the wrought-iron bars, but the storms had moved on. The moon shone in the window and lit the room in sharp contrasts of shadow and mother-of-pearl opalescence. It was a landscape of blacks and whites and grays in which both of them looked to have the same neutral shade of skin. In the mirror above the bureau, Zolotow watched Kendra pull her damp T-shirt off over her head. She scrounged in a drawer for a clean one, the moon painting her long legs, smooth flanks, and white panties, highlighting the splines of her ribs and the muscles across her back. She pulled back the covers and climbed into bed beside him, wrapping one silken leg across his thighs and snuggling close. She was hurting his knee, but the marijuana had taken the edge off the pain. He found the strength to wrap his arm around her. He stroked her hair.

"First thing in the morning," he whispered, "I'll get us out of here."

Her hand brushed his cheek and came to rest on his broad chest. "Do you have anyone, Martin? A woman, I mean. Someone waiting for you back in California."

"In California? No."

She sensed the evasiveness of that answer. "Are you in love with someone?"

He smiled softly. "Usually."

"I see."

Silence reigned for several minutes. They could still hear the crackling of the barn fire through the thin walls of their prison. Had Kendra's room not been on the back side of the building, they'd have been able to see the glow of whatever was left. The wind moaned. Razor found something to bark at, out by the pig pens. Tumbleweeds, maybe.

"Is there someone you love more than anything, Martin? Someone you'd walk away with and never look back, not once, not even for all the tea in China?"

"I don't even drink tea."

She bit his shoulder.

"Okay. Sorry. There was someone. Once. She was in France last I heard."

"Oh. A French lady?" And he heard in her voice that she

wondered how she could possibly compare with that. She, a prostitute from Oklahoma. A black woman, at that. "What happened?" she asked.

"I don't know. Things didn't work out. I forget things, you know. Mixed cerebral dominance, they call it. My brain is wired funny. Left-handed and right-eyed when I'm not feeling out and out ambidextrous. The imaginative and logical halves of my brain carefully balanced. Sometimes the balance doesn't hold, and things just go haywire. Sometimes ... sometimes I can't seem to hold on to anything important ... and my life goes haywire."

"But this French lady, you were in love with her?"

"Yes."

"And will you ever love like that again?"

"I don't know. Most of the things I touch turn to shit. People have a habit of dying around me. I'm not a good person to hang out with." He let out a long sigh, shivering. "It's really cold in here."

She pulled the sheets to his neck and snuggled her soft body closer. "I know. I'm sorry. The thermostat's locked in a box." She kissed his neck. "Try to sleep, Martin."

"What about you?" he asked. "Do you have anyone special? You've mentioned your family several times."

"Well, my brothers are mostly dead. One's in prison. My father died of a stroke. Mama remarried and moved to Atlanta. I haven't seen her in five years. All in all, the Wilkes family just fell apart one day." She shivered, as if something cold had just crept up her spine. "What about your family?"

Zolotow bit his lip, stared at the ceiling, and didn't answer immediately. Sensing that she'd stumbled into a sensitive area, she held him and waited. Insects chirped just the other side of the thin walls. A coyote howled at the moon. One of the horses whinnied and Razor barked.

"I never knew my father," he said. "My mother's pretense was that she was an actress. She used to come home, talking about casting calls she had made and commercials she had done. We didn't have a television, so I never saw the commercials. It wasn't until I was much older that I knew that they never existed, leastwise not with her in them. She would talk about TV roles she was trying to score, about movies she hoped to be chosen for ... it was all a sham."

She stroked his cheek. "You don't know that, baby. Maybe she really was making those casting calls. In between, though, she had a child to feed. You know?"

"I know." He caught her hand and kissed her palm. "One day her pimp came in and started in on her with a blackjack. I was seven years old. When I tried to help, the pimp split my skull open. When I was finally released from the hospital, the State took me away from her and put me in a foster home. I never saw her again. I ran away from more than one of those homes and I went looking, but I never found her."

She didn't say anything. She just held him. She'd seen more than her share of life's misery, and she knew there were no words to explain it or make it bearable. You simply endured. Nothing else worked.

"Go to sleep," she finally whispered, her breath tickling his ear.

"I've a confession to make first."

"It doesn't matter. Go to sleep. It's after four in the morning."

"It's important," he told her. "What I said earlier ... when I promised I'd get you out of this " He swallowed the lump in his throat. "I don't think I can keep that promise, Kendra. I honestly don't."

"I know," she whispered.

He slept then, snoring softly, flinching as his body remembered the day's events. Kendra held him and, when she was certain he was really asleep, she cried, her tears pooling in the moonlight that touched his shoulder. Later, while she slept, too, several of the girls snuck into the room and crawled into bed with them. When the bed was full, more of them brought in their pillows and their blankets, and slept on the floor. About five-thirty, a loud noise woke them.

"What's that?" he asked.

"Helicopter," whispered Rayleen, snuggled against his

back.

"Help?" He was thinking of his email, hoping Hector had read it and sent the National Guard to Beaver to find him.

"No," said Kendra. "It's one of McDevitt's club members ... come for the hunt. Go back to sleep, Martin."

And he did. Sometime before the sun came up, he dreamed about tumbleweeds and vampires. The tumbleweeds all looked like Razor and growled whenever he tried to touch Kendra. The vampires carried baseball bats and intravenous bags of blood. When he tried to run, his legs wouldn't work. Debbie was there, mocking his weak attempts to flee. She leaned close, close enough that he could feel her hair on his face and smell her perfume, and she whispered, *You're nobody's fucking white knight, Martin Zolotow.*

Zolotow woke with Kendra's hand beside his face, her wrist watch just inches away. Squinting, he brought it into focus. 8:16. Morning had graffitied the wall at the foot of the bed with a giant tic-tac-toe pattern. He recognized it as the bars over the window. Oddly enough, he didn't wake with his usual "Where the hell am I?" feeling. For once, he knew exactly where he was. It was as if the impending day, a day he expected to witness his death, would be gifted with stunning clarity.

In this state, he lay there and went over the things that he knew. Washington and McDevitt were into illegal, designer drugs. Washington was probably on the distribution end of things. When McDevitt's business needs changed slightly, to a requirement for young African-American women, it would only be natural to approach Washington as a supplier for said requirements. McDevitt had somehow acquired expertise in genetics, through the mysterious Dr. Alahandro perhaps. They were working toward creating what Daryl Johnson called a synthetic telomerase, the key to lengthening the telomere, the key to immortality. Such an endeavor would take a considerable amount of funding. Zolotow guessed that the mysterious Coon Hunters were, in fact, McDevitt's financial backers. But something had backfired. The Coon Hunters thought they were vampires and they were, if Coop was any indication, dying. Beauchamps was some sort of key to a cure. Zolotow guessed that he had been another guinea pig, possibly a successful one. They hadn't needed information from the man. All they'd needed was a tissue sample. He suddenly recalled Johnson saying something about African-Americans having a DNA proclivity for telomerase production. If Beauchamps had been a guinea pig, then his modified DNA must hold this secret. Johnson had also said the DNA proclivity was strongest in black females. Well, the Coon Hunters had an obvious preference for them. And Kendra had said that none of those hunted by the Coon Hunters ever came back. After having seen what McDevitt did to Johnson, Zolotow had no trouble believing that.

A shadow destroyed the pattern on the wall. A long, leggy shadow, with full breasts and long, wavy hair. Zolotow raised his head and smiled at the beauty standing by the window. A pale pink T-shirt, minus the sleeves and most of the midriff. White cotton panties. Eyes as black as midnight. Skin like hot cocoa. Legs like a gazelle's. He could easily imagine this girl running track or playing a mean game of hoops. He didn't do a head count, but it looked like most of the women were here in this one room, crowded into the bed with him, sleeping all over the floor. A smorgasbord of earthly delights. They were all asleep except for the tall, dark beauty by the window.

"Good morning," he said, just loud enough for her to hear. "See anything out there?"

"A rainbow," she answered.

"Think you could help me out of bed so I can see it, too ... uh —" He couldn't remember her name, but he recognized her as the one who'd given him the marijuana. He wondered if she had more.

"Penny," she said, crossing the room. "Here, give me your hands." She tried to help him crawl over Rayleen and Tessa, the two girls between him and one side of the bed, but it was too painful for him. She wound up making them crawl over him, while he slid on his back to the edge of the bed. Tessa giggled at Zolotow's typical morning condition. She actually caused him to blush when she gave him a friendly squeeze as she crawled over.

Rayleen didn't wake up enough to notice anything. After the crossing, she burrowed up against Kendra and went to snoring as loud as any man Zolotow had ever known.

"A long time ago," he gasped between clenched teeth as Penny pulled him to a seated position on the edge of the bed, "I was run down by a crazy woman in a Ford Mustang. I tell you, Pretty Penny, that was a walk in the park compared to this."

Though she hardly seemed embarrassed by his nakedness, he gathered the towel around his waist and tied it tight. Then he put his arm around her and she helped him hobble to the window. Flat prairie, as far as the eye could see. He could count the trees on one hand. Hardly the sort of terrain in which one would prefer to be hunted. There was a corral that he'd missed last night in the dark and several horses munching on the sparse prairie grass. There were some small mounds in the distance that he guessed belonged to prairie dogs. And the ever-popular tumbleweeds. The rainbow, as colorful and vivid as a third grader's water color painting, touched down on the prairie just beyond the horses and the horizon. There was probably a pot of gold there, if he could only get out of this prison.

"It's beautiful, isn't it?"

He smiled at Penny. "Yeah, it is. Sometimes, during the storm, you forget there'll be a rainbow afterward." He squeezed her hand. "Thanks."

He turned away from the window and spotted the crutch leaning against the bedroom door.

"McDevitt," Penny explained. "He's waiting in the kitchen. I thought I'd give you a minute to appreciate the rainbow before I ruined your morning."

She helped him to the crutch. From there, he was able to make his own way down the hallway to the kitchen, one arm on the crutch, the other braced against the wall. McDevitt was at the table, a Beretta 92 beside his coffee cup. Two of the girls were seated in the living room, watching the news. The announcer was talking about last night's storm. The Oklahoma panhandle hadn't seen that much rain since 1932. The Beaver and Goff Rivers had swollen over their banks and taken a great toll on local livestock and crops. Several tornadoes had touched down in Guymon, where a trailer park had been destroyed and two people were killed.

"Your average trailer park," said McDevitt, "acts like a tornado magnet. You'd think, by now, Oklahomans would understand that."

Zolotow hobbled over and took a seat at the table. "Morning," he said to the girls, though he couldn't recall either of their names. They looked too frightened to respond. Penny poured him a cup of coffee.

"Freshen that for me, Penny," McDevitt said, extending his own cup. He sniffed at Zolotow. "My, don't you smell purty!" The bald crown of his head wrinkled obscenely as he made a face. His sharpened canines, hooked over his lower lip, lent him a gargoyle-like appearance.

The news cut to an old farmer in Turpin who'd lost half his hogs to a flash flood. "I guaran-damn-tee ya," said the farmer, his lower lip packed with snuff, "they ain't been this much rain in these here parts since prohibition. My poor hawgs was treading water, bellering for help, for a good hour 'fore they just plain tuckered out and went under." There were flash flood warnings out for Beaver, Harper, and Woodward Counties and a second storm front was expected to pass through within the next 24 hours.

"You missed all the good stuff," McDevitt said, sipping his coffee. "Their opening piece was all about the strange goings-on in Beaver. Seems several vehicles and a sheriff's car were found wrecked along 270. The sheriff's missing. There was blood — a lot of blood — but no bodies. Two of the vehicles were unlicenced, but the other two were from OKC. They're trying to run them down now, but panhandle law enforcement ain't the most efficient you've ever seen. One of the OKC vehicles was equipped with ankle cuffs in the back seat. Kinky, eh?"

Zolotow sipped his coffee and held his tongue.

"Well, you're looking a bit more rested anyway. It was certainly a busy day for you, Zolo." McDevitt set his coffee cup on the table. There was something about the lack of facial hair, the missing eyebrows, that lent his face a particularly sinister demeanor when he smiled. "Tell me, what'd you think of the lab?"

Zolotow shrugged. "Looked impressive enough."

McDevitt nodded. "Yeah, it should. Cost me enough money. Lots of activity in there today. People making sure you didn't fuck with anything."

"People running experiments on Beauchamps' arm," Zolotow speculated.

"There you go being a detective again, Zolo."

"Sorry. Old habit."

"I imagine Johnson fed you enough to put some things together. Amazing, isn't it? Everything you are, everything I am, it's all coded in our DNA. And our DNA actually decides when our bodies give up the fight against entropy." He chuckled. "God damn, I like that word. Entropy. Say it with me, Zolo. Entropy."

Zolotow sipped his coffee.

"Entropy," said Kendra from the hallway. Her hair was messed up and the pillow had left marks on one left side of her face, but Zolotow thought she was beautiful. She'd found a pink bathrobe that made her look positively domestic. Strangely enough, Zolotow was pleased to see her lovely flesh hidden from McDevitt's eyes. She shuffled into the kitchen, rubbing at her eyes.

"Those are the cutest fuzzy pink slippers I've ever seen," Zolotow told her.

She smiled at him. "Thanks, hon."

"I'd known about that pink bathrobe, though, I'd have probably worn it myself. You don't know how out of sorts I feel walking around in nothing but a towel."

She patted his cheek, stroked his bare shoulder. "Pink's not really your color, love. Penny, would you get me some coffee?"

"Sure, Kendra."

Throughout this chit-chat, in the back of his mind, Zolotow was debating whether he could move fast enough with the crutch to knock the gun away from McDevitt's hand. He'd still be faced with the same problem as last night: hand-to-hand, he was no match for the man. But maybe one of the girls could get to the gun.

McDevitt looked from Zolotow to Kendra and back again, his brow knit and his ghost eyes squinted. "I'll be goddamned! You have got some stones, Zolo. You actually dipped your wick in that last night, didn't you? Holy shit! After all you been through, you still had time for a pony ride. I am impressed."

"You're as crude as you are bald," Zolotow muttered.

"Well, that may be true, but you know what, dipshit? I aim to be crude and uncivilized for a long fucking time. The secret's in my DNA. It's in yours, too, but you don't know how to unlock it. Take a moment to consider what I'm talking about here, Zolo." McDevitt picked up the Beretta and hugged it against his chest as if he sensed the temptation the gun was causing. "There are cells that don't age. Not ever. The sperm cells you so happily doused this nigger bitch with last night will die, but only because of their environment. In the right environment, they would multiply and live forever. Sperm cells don't age. Isn't that absolutely fucking incredible?"

"How and when we die isn't important," said Zolotow. "It's what we do with our lives that —"

"Oh, horseshit! You got that from some fucking movie." McDevitt leaned across the table, the gun so close that Zolotow could smell the oil on it. "There's this little single cell amoeba-like something or another thing called a tetrahymena. Like a fucking worm or something, I dunno. It lives forever, Zolotow. Can you imagine that? Sure, you can kill it, but it doesn't age like we do. It's immortal." He leaned back in his chair. "Now you tell me, what makes it right for that fucking worm to live forever and me to live less than a hundred years? The difference is in our DNA. And if we can alter ours ... Man! I'll gladly trade a few side effects, like no body hair, for immortality. Science is fucking awesome, ain't it?"

"When used properly, yes."

"I watched both my parents grow old and die, Zolo. I have no desire to join them. My Daddy was one of the richest men in Ohio. Built a farm machinery business from nothing. My Daddy sold more fucking tractors than any other man in the world.

But you know, none of it was worth a damn to him on the day he checked out. Everything was handed over to me, when I'd never done a thing to earn it. What the hell was the point in accumulating all that wealth, eh?"

Zolotow didn't even bother trying to hide his yawn.

"I tell you, he literally worked himself to death. Every day of the week except Saturdays. On Saturdays, his buddies would come over and they'd hunt coon. This was in Licking Valley, Ohio, Zolo. I'm sure you never heard of the place. They called themselves the Licking Valley Coon Hunters Club. I watched all those men grow old, just like my Daddy. Got to the point where they couldn't hit a coon if you hung it on the end of their rifle, but they kept getting together, kept tromping through the woods ... right up to the day they were all buried there. Old age, who needs it? I took Daddy's money and moved to the most unlikely place in the country, after Licking Valley, of course. From here, I've waged my war on old age. And I'm this —" He held up two fingers, tightly space. "— fucking close to kicking its ass."

The room had gone quiet. The girls in the living room had even turned off the television. McDevitt scratched his nose with the barrel of the Beretta.

"I'm rambling, aren't I? Boring the shit out of the lot of ya?" McDevitt chuckled. "Hell, might as well cut to what I really came down here for." He reached into a pocket of his coveralls and pulled out the Polaroid picture of Debbie. He laid it on the table between them. "Who's this?"

Zolotow shrugged. "Beats the hell out of me."

"That so? Well, I talked to Earl this morning before coming over here. He was out slopping the hogs. Not a job Earl's particularly fond of, but as you recall I set him the task of taking care of that messiness out on the highway last night. Anyway, he says you know this little girl. He says Washington threatened to kill her if you didn't get his daughter back for him."

"What's your point?"

"My point? Well, damn, Zolo, I figured a smart detective like you would see something like this coming. I figure the easiest thing for you to smell is the shit you done stepped in. Why didn't you tell me all this shit yesterday? You coulda saved us a whole lot of grief. See, according to Earl, Washington's got this guy Herman Munch, also know as Bruiser, watching over this little sweetie. Hell, Zolo, I know Bruiser! I coulda just called him up, told him to lay off, and sent you back home, no harm done!

"Course, that was yesterday ... 'fore you stepped all in this shit."

McDevitt reached into his coveralls again and pulled out a cell phone. "Hell, Bruiser and I are old friends." He dialed a number. "We grew up together in Ohio. Like I told you: Licking Valley, Ohio. Most beautiful place on Earth. We wanted to go into professional wrestling together. He actually did wrestle for a couple years, but then it turned out he had really bad knees. I changed my mind as soon as I was old enough to realize it was all fake. What the hell's the point if you don't really get to hurt the other guy?"

Someone picked up on the other end. "Herman? Yeah, it's me, Jimmy McDevitt. Hey, you old cocksucker, when did you start working for niggers? Toby Washington, that's the nigger I'm talking about, you limp dick motherfucker. What's he paying you? Ah, shit, Bruise, you're worth more than that. I hate to see you running errands for coons. Listen, pack your shit and come to Oklahoma, pard. I'll put you to work. Yeah? Great."

McDevitt suddenly aimed the Beretta at Zolotow's head. "Listen, Bruise, this Debbie something or other that you're supposed to be keeping an eye on? Yeah, that's right, the one Toby's got you watching. Listen. Plug her. Yeah, now. Go on and take her out. Fuck Toby Washington! You work for me now. Sure. Mom, dad, the whole fucking family. Kill em all and then head on up here so we can talk over old times. You too, man. Bye."

McDevitt hung up and slipped the phone back in his pocket. "There. That takes care of all your worries, Zolo. I didn't want your mind occupied with trivial bullshit when it came time for the hunt, see? If you were worried about that jail bait in Dallas, you might not be concentrating on your basic escape tactics and survival skills. I want your mind clear. Any other calls we need to make? Anybody else know you're vacationing in Oklahoma?"

Zolotow said nothing. He just sat there, unblinking, staring into McDevitt's eyes.

"You're a real piece of work, Jimmy," said Kendra, but McDevitt ignored her.

McDevitt chuckled. "Is this where you surge up out of your chair, all maniacal like, and try to beat the shit outta me, Zolo? I think we did that scene last night." He waited for a reaction. When he got none, he pushed back his chair and stood up. "I've got to run over to the lab and see if Alahandro's latest magic juice is ready for Brother Cooper. That boy makes one hell of a guinea pig." He paused by the door. "You just make yourself comfortable until I send someone after you, Zolo." Then he was gone, the door locking tight behind him.

Kendra reached out and took Zolotow's hand. "I'm sorry about your friend."

"At least he didn't know about the email I sent last night. I've got to hope that Garza's on his way to Dallas. Maybe he's already there. If I allow myself to concentrate on Debbie, who I can't possibly help, then I'm useless to all of you."

Kendra bit her lip and said nothing.

"What do we do now?" Penny asked. The other women crowded into the hallway, sleepy-eyed and mussed.

"Did you ever watch that TV show, *MacGyver*?" Zolotow asked. "Well, this is that point in the show where MacGyver would go through the kitchen cabinets and put together something that would save the day."

The women just stared at him.

"I don't suppose we have a chemist in the house?"

"How many of you will they take?" Zolotow asked. He'd gotten dressed (returning Debbie's photo to his pants pocket) and they'd fed him eggs and toast again. Tessa had located some pain killers for him. He'd taken four of the pills with a shot of Jack Daniels. Rose had come up with the JD, one last swallow in the bottom of a bottle one of her companions had left one night.

She'd been saving it for a special occasion.

"Three or four," said Penny. She was standing at the kitchen window, looking out at the yard. "There are two limos and one helicopter out front. That's three visitors. Plus Jimmy will probably want to hunt."

Zolotow didn't want to comment on the fact that McDevitt had already hunted last night or that the crazy bastard probably intended to hunt him. "There's no way to know who they'll pick?"

"Well, we know they plan to pick me," Kendra interjected.

Zolotow squeezed her hand. "You won't be alone." He looked at the girls crowded around the kitchen table, saw the fear and the hope in their eyes. It unnerved him, that many eyes watching to see what he would say next. He'd spent most of his adult life alone, answering to no one. Sure, there had been a lot of women in his life, but few that had been around for long. Responsibility for others had always been a transient experience at best. And he'd certainly never been responsible for so many. He let out a long sigh.

"Okay, we need to arm ourselves," he told them. "I need all of you to start thinking. I need you to find anything and everything that could possibly be used as a weapon. Because we'll have to conceal these weapons before they come back, every one of you will need to have something hidden, in case you're one of the ones who gets picked."

"But we don't have any weapons," one of them protested.

"Yes you do," he countered. He pointed to the framed print in the living room. "Break that glass. Wrap the longest pieces in strips of bed sheet so you can hold them like a knife. Hide them under your sleeves or your pants leg." He looked about some more. "That lamp. Rip off the cord and use it as a garrote."

"A what?"

He demonstrated in the air with an imaginary cord. "Takes some strength, though. Perhaps I should take the garrote."

Taneesha dug in the silverware drawer and came up with several butter knives.

"That's good," Zolotow told her. "Find something to sharpen the edges on."

Rayleen showed him a pump bottle of hair spray. "Would this work? Like mace?"

"Maybe." He suddenly remembered the eggs he'd eaten. "Judy, where's that cayenne pepper? Open the hair spray and dump in the pepper. Mix it up real good. Instant pepper spray."

The girls scrounged through their rooms. One of them brought him several pencils. Another brought him a broom. He told them to break the broom handle into three pieces.

"Sharpen them with the glass from the picture. If they think they're vampires, then we'll put stakes through their hearts."

One of the girls came up with a roll of Scotch tape that had been used for wrapping presents. They used the tape to strap broom handle stakes, pencils, and shards of glass under their clothing. Zolotow tied the lamp cord around his waist under the white lab coat. He shaved the tip of his crutch down to a crude point, then concealed it under the rubber cap. Like the broom handle, he thought it was the perfect weapon for vampires.

"Does everyone have a weapon?" he asked when they were finished. The girls were crowded around the kitchen table where he sat. They all nodded. Most of them had more than one weapon. "Kendra, show me what you've got."

"Why, Martin, is that any way to talk to a lady?" she responded coyly. The other girls laughed, but Zolotow only frowned. He was in no mood for jokes. He'd gone deadly serious on them, his mood driven by the fact that he suddenly felt all their lives hanging in his hands.

"Oh, all right," Kendra huffed.

She had peeled back the carpet in a corner of the living room and sharpened a butter knife against the concrete floor. The blade now had a decent edge and the blunt tip had been filed to a point. The knife was taped to her ankle, beneath her jeans.

"Good," Zolotow told her. "Now, listen carefully to me. All of you. Squeamishness ends here, in this room. These men will kill you. You must not hesitate to hurt — or even kill them first. You go for eyes, throats, whatever soft targets they present you with. You strike and you get away from them. Understand?"

They nodded.

"The element of surprise will be in your favor. They're expecting to be the hunters in this game — they're used to being the hunters but we're going to turn things around. I need you to strike first, strike fast, and strike with lethal intent. There's no other way to get through this. Understand?"

They nodded again, but he saw something less than conviction in most of their eyes.

Zolotow wished he had a powerful story to tell them, something inspiring. He had nothing. His mind was a blank. He recognized his mind set for what it was. He was clearing his head of everything. Soon, the only thing he wanted himself thinking of was survival. Whatever that took, he must do it. They had to be willing to do the same. He didn't know any better way to get that across to them.

"Anybody got any cards?" he asked, finally. "It might be a long time before they come for us?"

So they played poker, the girls teasing him by betting sexual favors to be paid in full when he recuperated. He called their bets with Cadillacs and Beamers that he didn't own and could never afford. In between hands, he would slip in things like "You can't hesitate to strike first" and "Don't stop with one thrust, you pull your knife or pencil or whatever you have out, and you plunge it in again and again." The fear in the girls' eyes didn't go away, but it didn't get any worse. "These are men," he told them, "bigger and stronger than you. The one thing you don't want to do is wrestle with them. You slip in, hurt them as bad as you can, and slip out of reach. Don't let them grapple with you." As he talked, some of the combat fever he was feeling build within himself began to show in their eyes, accentuated by their fear.

They ate sandwiches for lunch. Zolotow tried to eat light and advised them to do the same. They kept watch on the front yard, afraid more limos or helicopters might show up as the day progressed. None did. They watched television. The twelve o'clock news reported that one of the OKC vehicles involved in last night's mystery was a rental car checked out to one Daryl Wayne Johnson, an OKC resident and student at OU. Like the county sheriff, Johnson's whereabouts were unknown. He'd last been seen filling up the car with gas in Woodward.

The sky remained overcast, the morning's rainbow quickly torn apart by high prairie winds and fast-moving, black clouds. The weatherman out of Guyman was calling for more rain. The likelihood of further tornadoes was high. The entire panhandle was under a flash flood warning.

It was nearly five o'clock by the time someone came for them. When the front door opened, Zolotow was surprised to see that it was Coop. The pale scarecrow of a man was seated in a wheelchair, an IV line in his neck (perhaps the last place for a viable vein), and he was flanked by three men with shotguns. The only color to his face was the broken capillaries in his cheeks and the livid bruises Zolotow had left. Even Coop's eyes seemed to have gone pale and lifeless, their malamute blue now a muted off-white.

Coop cleared his throat and surveyed the kitchen. He looked miserable. He looked like a refugee from a terminal illness hospice. Zolotow was reminded of his initial assessment, that the man was dying of AIDS. "Jimmy sent me," Coop announced rather flatly, "to pick who gets hunted." He made the men with the shotguns wait outside, over their protests, and closed the door behind him.

Zolotow slid his chair back from the kitchen table, but remained seated. Though he'd been flexing the bad leg off and on for the entire day, so that it wouldn't be too terribly stiff when he needed it, he'd also been conserving his strength, giving his body as much time as possible to heal. "You don't look so good, Coop."

Coop thumped the IV bottle hanging from the back of his wheelchair. "New juice. Special Beauchamps concoction. Not sure if it's curing or killing me, though. My stomach's in knots and my head feels like a balloon."

"Your mama never told you to just say no, Coop?"

"Mama never told me I might live forever, Zolo."

"Right now," Zolotow replied, "you look like you'll be

lucky to last the week."

Coop shrugged. "Jimmy's lab rats have had their set backs. Some of the first guys to take the treatments have died. A couple, like me, aren't looking so good. But later treatments, like the one Jimmy took himself, have had very few side effects. We think the batch that Beauchamps got was the real deal." He stroked his IV bag again. "If it works, I'll be just fine. You're looking at the cure for damn near everything."

"Except maybe poor taste in music," Zolotow said.

Coop scowled at him and surveyed the girls, his eyes all squinted up behind his thick glasses. The crow's feet radiating from the corner of his eyes looked like bloodless cuts running all the way to the bone. His gaze stopped with Kendra. "Kendra Washington, is it?" He chuckled. "Hope she paid you plenty to take her place, hon."

Rayleen stepped forward. "I'll go in my own place." Her face had gone so pale that her mulatto freckles had all but vanished. Her lower lip quivered and her hands were clenched tight behind her as if she thought they were the only thing to give away her fear, but her head was up and she met Coop's ghostly gaze without flinching. Zolotow was proud of her.

Coop chuckled. "Jimmy sent me to pick someone. He didn't send me to ask for volunteers. You're the only safe one here, Rayleen. I figure I might need you later. Sit down." The poor girl just stood there, wringing her hands, an odd mix of anger, fear, and relief on her face. Silent tears sprang from her eyes and trailed down her cheeks.

"We could still figure out a way to take her back to Washington," Zolotow suggested.

"What's this *we* shit? You're going to be dead in an hour or two."

"You'd better hope so, Coop."

"Shit. I know so." Then he scanned the room, counting girls. Your average redneck, Zolotow noted, is incapable of counting without moving his lips. "Penny," Coop said at last, "you have got the longest, most beautiful legs I have ever seen, darling. You remember what you told me when I said I wanted to slip between them?"

Penny got up from the living room sofa. "I told you I'd take my legs and crush the life out of you, break your scrawny toothpick spine in two, before you ever slipped a millimeter of your little one inch dick in me."

"Ouch," Zolotow snickered.

"Well, hon, you just got picked." Coop smiled at her. Penny merely shrugged her shoulders and went to stand beside Zolotow, one hand on his shoulder.

Coop pulled at his lips, scratched at the stubble on his chin. "Taneesha."

"No!" cried several of the other girls. The color drained from Taneesha's cheeks and throat. Instantly, she acquired twenty years of hard-living, gathered in her eyes and straddling her shoulders. For a moment, she looked like she was going to collapse. Her hands went to her chest and lay there against her breasts, shaking like leaves in a storm.

Zolotow got to his feet, leaning on the crutch. "She's got kids at home, Coop. Pick someone else."

"I'll go," said Rose.

"Or me," said Tessa.

Coop rolled back to the door and pulled it open. "Let's go." The three men with shotguns crowded into the kitchen.

"I said pick someone else," Zolotow growled.

Coop rolled his chair out the door. "If they don't follow, start shooting," he told the men with the shotguns.

The western skyline was thick with black clouds. Lightning flickered somewhere beyond the front, too distant to hear. The wind coming off the prairie was ripe with the stench of pigs and, significantly less potent, the ozone odor of the approaching storm. Coop's wheelchair bogged down in the mud of the yard. He made one of the three gunmen push him. The other two gunmen flanked Zolotow and the three women, their twelve gauges trained primarily on the detective. The Mercedes and several other vehicles were scattered about the front yard, along with the two black limos and the helicopter. There were several men loitering on the front porch of the house, limo drivers maybe, perhaps even the pilot of the chopper.

"I don't get it," Zolotow told Coop. "I think I grasp the need for blood ... something to do with maintaining the synthetic telomerase in your body. But I don't understand the hunt. I don't understand murdering these innocent women."

Coop shrugged his bony shoulders without bothering to look back from the wheelchair. They were passing the house. Razor came out as if he intended to greet Kendra, but when he saw the gunmen, he backed off, growling. "Partly, Jimmy's just a fucking psycho, Zolo. You can't expect everything to make sense. True genius has its own insanity."

"That's a load of crap."

"Well, you asked me. If you ask Jimmy — and he was inclined to answer — he'd tell you he was building a race of supermen. Maybe he thinks he's Hitler or something. He'd say if you built a race of immortals, you want them to be loyal to you. Loyalty is sort of a primal thing, and the hunt is as primal as it gets. It's a brotherhood. Damn near religious. You heard him call me Brother Cooper yesterday. There's a bonding, a certain something that's shared through having slaughtered and fed off the innocents."

"Ask me, you're a bunch of sick bastards," Kendra muttered.

Coop ignored her. "Maybe it's caused by the genetics? Jimmy says the changes awake man's primal self. The reptilian mind and all that."

"Do you believe that?"

"I dunno. Jimmy's had plenty of financial backers and guinea pigs who've taken the treatments and *not* participated in his hunts. I hunted with him twice and really wasn't much good at it. So, most of the blood I've drank came from an IV bag. Even then, I'm not fond of it. Nasty shit sticks in the back of your throat, all thick and gooey, and you feel like you're gonna choke — it's like it just won't go down. I wash it down with a bottle of Miller Lite myself. Jimmy doesn't like that. He thinks I'm weak. If I wasn't one of his prize test subjects, I expect I'd already be pushing up daisies somewhere."

Which is why, Zolotow realized, Coop had tried to arrange a deal with Washington. With his daughter safe, Washington could have been persuaded to wipe out McDevitt and take over the operation. Washington would have owed Coop, and Coop would have worked to make sure that the cure — or, more precisely, a stable telomerase with no side effects — was found. He had what he needed to start. He had Beauchamps' arm. As someone who'd brought Washington's daughter back, he stood more of a chance of being taken care of than he did as just another of McDevitt's guinea pigs.

"Course, you destroyed our last shipment of blood. If I regain enough strength from this Beauchamps cocktail, I suppose I'll be thinking about hunting. Thanks to you, there's nothing else around here to drink." Coop smiled, his cheeks stretched as thin as a condom. Sunlight gleamed from his broken tooth. "Course, it's hard to hold down one of these squirming women and not spill your beer."

Zolotow refrained from bashing Coop's head in with his crutch, but he made a silent promise that Coop wouldn't be around to do any hunting when the day was over.

They passed the house and continued north past the lab. Kendra was walking beside Zolotow. Penny and Taneesha followed, Taneesha sobbing and Penny trying to comfort her. Beyond the lab lay the prairie, as barren and desolate as any terrain Zolotow had ever seen. Near the horse corral, there was a group of men, most of them relaxing in lounge chairs, drinking beer and watching the clouds roll in. There were a couple of coolers surrounded by scattered, empty beer cans. A radio was playing country music. Five more men with shotguns and two with hunting rifles flanked the whole ensemble. Earl was there, sitting on a cooler, whittling away at a stick with his pocket knife.

McDevitt broke from the group to meet them.

"You didn't start the party without us?" Zolotow asked.

"Of course not, Zolo. You and the ladies are, after all, a very essential element to this evening's proceedings. Care for a beer?"

Zolotow shrugged. "You're not worried it'll thin my blood?"

McDevitt laughed. "You're a funny man, Zolotow. I'd have liked to have known you under different circumstances. I bet we would have been great friends."

"I bet I would have cut your throat in your sleep."

McDevitt shrugged. His bald head glistened with sweat. Zolotow wondered how he kept the sweat out of his eyes without eyebrows. He was going to ask, but the men in the lawn chairs got to their feet, capturing Zolotow's attention.

Zolotow leaned close to Kendra. "The guy on the left ... is that who I think it is?"

"Yeah. The Reverend Willy Willis himself. Straight from the Pearly Gates to Beaver, Oklahoma."

Televangelist Willy Willis wasn't as well known as Falwell or Oral Roberts, but he was rapidly making progress. He'd made a life of convincing sinners that they could buy their way into Heaven — with Willis as broker, of course. Charismatic, with a voice that was hauntingly close to Jack Kennedy's, Willis could capture and hold an audience. He'd started out doing tent revivals throughout the Carolinas and Georgia, terrorizing rural communities with fire and brimstone lectures to rival anything in the *Old Testament*. Three years of that taught him what worked and what got him run out of town. In that time, he built a solid crew of born-again sinners whose affirmations to Christ could wring a tear (and a buck) from the most hardened of men. Throw in a *Playboy* Playmate of the Year, who Willis not only saved from a life of softporn films and debauchery, but eventually married, a boys choir that could sing like angels, a troupe of actors who could perform admirably with and without their crutches, wheelchairs, walkers, dialysis machines, and so on, and the *Reverend Willy Willis World Rejuvenation of Faith* was officially off and running. His first year, he was on three stations in Georgia and Alabama. The following year, stations in the Carolinas, Tennessee, and Mississippi picked up the show. Cable came next and suddenly Willis was coast to coast, passing the plate on Sunday mornings and afternoons, as well as Wednesday and Saturday nights.

Now Zolotow knew where some of that money had gone.

"And you recognize the guy beside him, right?" Kendra whispered.

Zolotow nodded. He did recognize him, though he couldn't remember the guy's name. It was something rugged. Something that sounded like a firearm. Colt something or other. Remington maybe. Winchester Browning Magnum ... or something equally ridiculous. He'd had a brief career on some football team, had gone from there to infomercials for exercise equipment and health food supplements, and then ultimately landed a role starring in a low budget action flick. Somehow, perhaps because the story had been above par, even if the acting wasn't, the movie had gone on to make a decent return and, in short order, the guy had starred in three sequels and guest appearances on half a dozen TV shows. He might not be much of an actor, but he was ruggedly handsome, had the physique of a bodybuilder without all the offensive, excessive, bulging veins, and Zolotow had heard more than one lady friend make the comment that he had the cutest ass ever bared to a camera (this during a guest appearance on *NYPD Blue*).

"Brett Caliber," Kendra supplied. "To think I would have loved to jump his bones at one time."

"Play your cards right and maybe you still can," Zolotow replied. The third club member was a mystery to him.

"That's our esteemed Governor, the Honorable Jerry Jeff Watson," Kendra said. "The big stink this last year was a sexual harassment scandal that he managed to sidestep. Bet the voters would love to know what he's up to now."

Watson was a squinty-eyed, wisp of a man, no more than five four, a hundred and forty pounds if he wore heavy shoes, a wool sweater, and kept his briefcase in hand when he got on the scales. His hair was thin and straw-colored, receding and blow-dried. He was cultivating what he probably hoped would one day be a mustache. How he'd risen to Governor of Oklahoma was a mystery to Zolotow. He didn't look like the sort to instill voter confidence. Perhaps he'd run unopposed. Every other politician in Oklahoma had gone fishing that day.

All three men appeared to be in infinitely better shape

than Coop. Whatever concoction they'd been subjected to in McDevitt's lab, it had reeked less havoc on their systems. Perhaps it had been a later derivative, something just short of what had worked on the late Beauchamps. These three men might be the last in a long series of experiments, preceded by Coop and McDevitt himself. Still, all three men showed some signs of what they'd attempted to become. Caliber's hair was noticeably thinner than Zolotow recalled from the TV. It almost seemed as if the Oklahoma wind was stripping it from the man's scalp at that very moment. His eyes were watery and red and his hands shook with a palsy the cameras could never hope to hide. Willis had a twitch that cocked his neck and twisted his lip every ninety seconds or so. He was pale enough to have just come from a personal session with God or the Devil, whichever one would deign to speak to such an utter waste of human flesh. Watson appeared to be just plain deteriorating. He might have never carried much muscle on his fragile frame, but surely he'd once been more than just skin and bones. He appeared to be leaning into the wind, his hawkish nose just asking to be broken by one of Kendra's karate kicks. Though none of the three had gotten around to filing their teeth — a decision based, no doubt, on their public appearances — all of them had a lupine look about them. It was something in the way they chewed their lips, something about the way they stood and the way their arms hung, something in the way they looked on the women and panted in a manner that went beyond prurient.

"I don't like this, Jimmy," Watson whined. "These storms blowing in. All that ruckus last night. Half the regulars not bothering to show up. And now, who's the guy with the crutch? What's he doing here?"

"Gentleman, this is Martin Zolotow."

Zolotow smiled and waved. "Howdy, bloodsuckers."

"What's he doing here?" Watson asked again.

"He's part of the hunt," McDevitt replied.

"Part of the hunt?"

McDevitt nodded. "I don't want you boys getting soft. You want the women, you go through him."

Caliber cracked his knuckles and, for a moment, adrenaline eradicated his shakes. There was something feral hiding behind his eyes. "Fine by me," he said, muscles tense, looking as if he were posing for a camera, "one lab technician with a crutch can't be much of a hassle."

Zolotow didn't bother explaining why he was wearing the lab coat. He vowed never to spend another dime on a Brett Caliber movie, though. "Now wait just a goddamned minute," said Reverend Willis. "I never agreed to —"

"No one asked what you agreed to, Brother Willis," McDevitt said coldly. "It's my game, gentleman. There are no customer options. No refunds. No try-it-before-you-buy-it. The rules of this game are whatever I say they are. You're either with me or you're dead. You're hunter or you're prey."

"This is bullshit," said the televangelist. "I paid you good money—"

"To enjoy things only I could give you," McDevitt finished for him. "You see here three lovely ladies. They're yours. All you have to do is hunt them down on the prairie. I think Mr. Zolotow would like to stop you. I suggest you kill him first."

Caliber leered, flexed his biceps some more. "Fine by me." Lightning flashed in the distance, setting a spark to his red-rimmed eyes.

"I don't know about this —" said Watson, his voice trailing off in a rumble of thunder.

McDevitt threw up his arms in mock exasperation. "Gentleman, can I let you go unchallenged week after week? Should I let you become as weak as the coon bitches you hunt? Zolo is the proverbial men-from-the-boys separator. He's the spice on your enchiladas. Quit your fucking whining and let's get on with it." He smiled at Zolotow and waved expansively at the barren prairie. "You have a twenty minute head start. North is your only authorized direction. The men with rifles are here to make sure you don't attempt to double back toward the highway. Turn south and they'll line you up in their cross hairs and shoot a leg out from under you."

Zolotow glanced down at his crutch. "That'd be rather redundant, wouldn't it?"

McDevitt snickered.

"You won't be coming along?" Zolotow asked.

"Not this time. Your young friend from last night was quite satisfying."

"Pity," Zolotow remarked. "You might have made it interesting."

McDevitt smiled. "You come back from this, and we'll make things as interesting as you like."

Zolotow returned the smile. "I'll do that."

"Clock's ticking," said Caliber.

Zolotow looked at the man, wondering if he was merely acting or if he really thought of himself as the rugged character he so often portrayed. "See you out there," he said. He tipped an imaginary hat to Earl as he passed. Earl merely flicked a wood shaving at him and smiled.

Zolotow led the three women out into the plains.

Interlude: "Why are you afraid to let anyone inside?"

Ellis was wearing her I'm-concerned-for-you face. It was a softer, more attractive look than her usual I-know-you're-crazy-and-I'm-going-to-prove-it, but Zolotow wasn't fooled. *First I tell you about my mother*, he thought, *and the next words you write in your report will be "Oedipus Complex." You'll say I sleep with prostitutes because my mother was one. In some dark corner of my mind, I'm really sleeping with her.* He had no doubt that she was just waiting to write some ground-breaking psychological profile for Martin Zolotow, the sort of shockingly revelational report that would get her promoted, the sort of thing that would get him a medical-based ticket out the door. So sorry, Zolo, but we're retiring you. You're too fucking looney to be walking around with a badge and a gun.

"You take these women off the streets," she coaxed, "help them put their lives back together, but then you always send them away. You never let them get inside your barriers. You never let down your guard, never let them see the real you. Why? Help me understand this, Detective Zolotow. Tell me what you're afraid of. What are the demons that you're hiding from?"

He suspected she knew nothing of demons. Safe in her tidy little office, peeking into the dirty little corners of other people's minds, she never got her own hands dirty. She lived in a bubble, as walled off as he, protected by dissertations on psychology and her own neatly wrapped morality. She might enjoy hearing about how her clients mucked around with the lowlifes and the slime, the dealers, pimps, whores, addicts, thieves, and murderers, but she'd never actually get close to them herself. Her territory was the warped minds of those tasked to take down the city's vermin. She drew the line at the vermin themselves. There was filth into which she wouldn't dare take a look.

"Show me one person who is close to you, Martin Zolotow."

"People who get close to me," he told her, honestly, "tend to wind up dead."

"Like Tony Saucier?"

He nodded, hiding his distaste for the direction today's session had suddenly taken. "Like Tony Saucier. Like three other partners before him."

Ellis pursed her lips. She took a moment to think about what she was going to say next, but that didn't make it any more palatable to Zolotow. "Some people in the department might think you're negligent when it comes to your partners." She slid her chair back several inches from whatever she saw flash in his eyes. Quickly, she added, "Of course, I don't think you would ever do anything intentional to endanger —"

"Without exception," he said, cutting her off, "my partners were my friends. Each of those men followed me into a bad situation, a situation in which I came out and they didn't. I couldn't have asked them to wait out those situations any more than they could have done so if they'd wanted to." He tried to swallow his anger, failed. "This job chews people up, Dr. Ellis. You know that. I've been chewed on plenty. I'm just too fucking mean for it to swallow.

"Instead ... it swallows those around me."

FIVE: *Rattlesnakes and Religion — Personal Space and Politicians — Swimming Pools and Movie Stars — Loyalty and Personal Equipment*

Twenty minutes out, Zolotow and the ladies came upon a gully that, on your normal panhandle day, would have been dry as a bone. However, the recent rainstorm had birthed a three foot wide, one foot deep creek (*what your average redneck would call a "crick,"* thought Zolotow) in the bottom of the gully. Penny speculated that somewhere, a dozen or more miles to the southeast, the creek emptied into the Beaver River, relieving the prairie of water that might otherwise foster the growth of something larger than a tumbleweed.

Zolotow didn't care so much about the geography of the creek as he did the opportunity it afforded them. He had no doubt that there was only one way to survive this evening: to confront the Reverend, the Governor, and the movie star, and walk away the victor. The gully afforded them with something he hadn't thought possible, a chance to lay an ambush. He wasn't fooling himself. Even if an ambush did allow them to kill the three hunters, they would ultimately be back in McDevitt's hands. But that was another day. Another chance to figure something out.

Behind them, the party of men were still visible against the white backdrop of the metal, prefab lab. The hunters were undoubtedly about to get underway, though it was hard to tell at this distance. To the southeast and southwest, the men with the hunting rifles were nearer, flanking them, making sure they didn't turn back. The gully was a deep gash in the flat epidermis of the panhandle, a ragged knife wound cut across their path northward.

"We get down in the creek bed," said Zolotow, "below the line of sight on this godforsaken prairie, out of sight of the guys with the high-powered rifles."

Kendra was hesitant. "I hate to throw cold water on your plans, honey, but don't you think the other girls tried this? Doesn't it seem a bit too convenient that we're given a twenty minute head start and that's just where we run across this gully?"

She was overlooking the fact that Zolotow had actually slowed the three of them down, but he saw what she was getting at. "You think we're doing exactly what they expect us to do?" He gestured helplessly. "I'm open to suggestions." A raindrop tickled the back of his neck. He imagined the men behind them, just getting started, holding out their hands to feel the first few drops of the coming storm. Willis and Watson would be complaining, cursing McDevitt and the rain, asking for raincoats or umbrellas. Brett Caliber would be thinking how good his muscles would look all slick and wet, as if the hunt were going to be captured on camera.

"We split up," Kendra suggested, with less conviction than he believed she hoped to convey. "Each of us takes a different tack northward, maybe we even get the chance to cut east or west at some point. There are three of them and four of us, so somebody isn't going to be followed. Simple math, that. Hopefully, that one person makes it out of here."

Zolotow shook his head. "Strength in numbers." He was thinking of Taneesha, who didn't look like she was ready to put up much of a fight. Kendra was fit and ready to run. Penny had the legs of a gazelle. But Taneesha was doomed. She looked like she couldn't run any faster than Zolotow himself. "We stick together. We use this creek to get out of sight. We look for a place to set up an ambush."

Kendra only shrugged her shoulders. The other two were willing to follow his lead.

The banks of the gully were a crumbling wash, tangled with tumbleweeds, slick red clay, strange pock-marked rocks that looked like some kind of iron ore, and even the bleached white skull of a steer. Zolotow was about to start down one of these washouts and into the gully when Penny caught his arm.

"Wait."

"What?"

She bent and picked up a rock, then tossed it into the tangle of brush in the washout. Something sinuous stirred beneath the brush. A distinctive, unmistakable sound followed the movement. Zolotow shivered. He couldn't think of a more frightening sound known to man. Using the crutch, he pushed away a tumbleweed, and there lay four feet of coiled terror.

"Just a little one," Penny said, "but he'd have damn sure bit you if you'd stepped on him."

The prairie rattler hissed, head back and ready to strike, twitching tail raised to issue that unique warning. Its back was criss-crossed with diamond-shaped markings. Its broad head quivered anxiously, forked tongue testing the air.

"Just go around him," Kendra said. "We're wasting time."

"No," said Zolotow, "I want him."

"You *want* him?"

"Yeah." Zolotow reversed his crutch and poked at the snake. The rattler responded by striking several times at the crutch, but quickly figured out that it couldn't hurt the hard maple. Uncoiling, it tried to escape toward the creek, but Zolotow pinned its head to the ground with the crutch. The snake writhed and twisted, its muscular body coiling about the crutch and wrenching it aside. The snake got loose twice this way before Zolotow finally got it pinned to the ground. He ran his hand along the twisting body and got hold of it. With his hand clamped strongly behind its broad head, he held the snake up for the women to see. All three stepped back. Taneesha hid behind Penny. The snake's body whipped about Zolotow's arm, struggling powerfully, the rattle at the end of its tail quivering desperately. The sound conveyed more anger now than warning. Zolotow got hold of its tail with his other hand and did his best to stretch the monster out straight and hold it still. The snake appeared to be nearly a match for his strength.

"I knew you were crazy," said Kendra.

"Still got your butter knife?" he asked.

"Why?"

"I need you to cut off its rattle."

She shook her head. "You've got the wrong girl, Zolo."

"Come on. Like you said, we're wasting time here. Take your knife and cut off its rattle."

"There's no fucking way I'm touching that snake!"

"Look," he said, "if you'd rather, you could hold its head while I cut off the rattle." For the first time, he sounded desperate, angry, afraid even. They had no idea how much holding the snake made his own skin crawl. To the best of his knowledge, nothing like this had ever slithered through L.A. He'd discovered one more reason to hate the Oklahoma panhandle.

"I'll do it," Penny said. She took the sharpened butter knife from Kendra and stepped forward. "Just don't let it go."

Zolotow smiled. "Furthest thing from my mind, love."

It wasn't as easy as he'd thought it would be. The snake doubled its exertions when Penny starting sawing at its tail. His knee began to ache part way through the operation and Zolotow was forced to sit with the snake in his lap. Blood flowed down the rippling snake and made his hand slippery where he was trying to hang on to its tail. "Hurry," he told Penny.

Finally, the rattle was free and the snake was mostly silent. It continued to hiss, a long, dry sound which raised the hair on the back of his neck. With each breath, the long, lean muscle that was its body flexed with mounting fury. A second later, it would twist and struggle in his hands, spreading bright red blood up and down the sleeves of his lab coat. Its eyes were hard and black, filled with more hatred than he'd ever seen. He thought of black holes in space, tiny specks of incalculable mass from which nothing could escape, not even light. The snake's eyes were like that.

Penny held up the rattle. "What do I do with this?"

"I don't care," Zolotow said. "Throw it away. I've got the half I wanted." He motioned for her to retrieve his crutch. "We need to get moving."

Penny slipped the rattle in her pocket, returned the knife

to Kendra, and helped Zolotow with his crutch. The snake twisted its body about the crutch, trying to use it for leverage to pull its head free of Zolotow's grip. It made walking difficult.

"Can we go now?" asked Kendra.

"Yeah. Come on. Down to the creek."

At the water's edge, he paused. His shoes sank into the brick-red mud. They'd left an obvious trail where they'd come down to the creek bed. It shouldn't take Tonto to trail them. A preacher, a politician, and an actor ought to do just fine. He also knew it would be obvious which tracks were his.

"Here's the plan," he said, glaring at Kendra. "We don't have time to discuss options. I figure they're fifteen minutes behind us, traveling together because we didn't separate. They'll come down the same wash that we took, following our trail. Penny, I want you to take Taneesha and head east from here. Stay low, out of sight, but stay out of the water. Walk in the mud where you'll leave lots of tracks. Kendra and I are going west. They'll split up to follow us, but we're only going to go west for about five minutes. After five minutes, we're going to double back, walking in the middle of the creek where we won't leave tracks. This will ultimately put us about ten minutes behind you two and about five minutes ahead of them. We're going to try and lay an ambush for whoever follows you two. We should have about ten minutes to take care of them before whoever originally went west figures out he's been duped. Okay?"

The three women nodded. For a minute, they stood there, none of them knowing what else to say. Finally, Zolotow waved the writhing snake at Penny and Taneesha, "Go on then, before I make you take the snake. Stay with the creek, and we'll catch up with you afterward."

Penny hesitated, looking like she wanted to say something. She took Taneesha by the arm and turned away, but not before she gave Zolotow a weak smile. *I'll see you later*, that smile said. *I'm trusting you to get us through this.* Zolotow felt something sour stir in the pit of his stomach.

The two women ran off down the creek bed, bent over so as to stay out of sight, slipping in the damp clay. As they ran away, Zolotow realized they were all soaked through, that it had begun to rain in earnest. Black clouds had captured the sun, bringing an early twilight. The wind was up. Raindrops stippled the surface of the creek and drowned out all other sound. Lightning set the bulbous clouds on fire.

He and Kendra turned and proceeded west along the water's edge. The crutch was more trouble than it was worth in the mud. He would have abandoned it, save for its value as a weapon. He finally relinquished it to Kendra for safekeeping and hobbled through the slippery mud with Kendra's help, though she kept jumping away each time the snake's struggles intensified. Five minutes bought them a mere 150 yards along the twisting bottom of the gully. Cursing, Zolotow debated proceeding on for another two or three minutes. A hundred and fifty yards was hardly enough distance to buy them the time they needed to dispatch whoever set out after Penny and Taneesha. One cry during the struggle and whoever had set out on the false trail would be alerted. They were running out of time, though, and it would have to do.

They splashed into the cold water and doubled back to the east. The water was red, thick with mud. There was no way even an expert tracker could peer into its depths and see the tracks they were leaving. The trick should work ... for the 150 yards they'd been able to carry it off.

Kendra frowned as they passed that point where they'd originally split from the other two women. Zolotow thought he knew what she was thinking: he'd wasted their time. He'd arbitrarily decided to place her in danger, giving the other two the best chance to escape. She might have been wondering if her chances hadn't been better before she'd found him in the barn. Things had been relatively quiet then, and she'd stood a good chance of escaping across the prairie before the hunt. She might have hiked down the road and hitched a ride somewhere safe. She might have found a farmhouse with a phone. Any number of things could have happened. Instead, she'd thrown in with him. Now, here she was, stuck in the very hunt she'd sought to avoid. Even had she stayed put, she'd have been better off not hooking up with him. There was always the chance she wouldn't have been picked. By helping him, she had guaranteed it. But she said nothing, blinking against the rain that was now coming down in buckets, flinching from the snake every time it twisted in his hands.

The creek slowed them down even more. Five minutes of trudging through the water yielded a hundred yards of distance from where they'd caught the rattler. Though the gully ran generally east and west, it was a winding path. For this reason, it was impossible to look back down the length of the creek and see the spot where the hunters would come down from the prairie. Though he wanted to, Zolotow refrained from peering above the rim of the gully in an attempt to get a look at their pursuers. The risk that they might spot him was too great. And there were the men with rifles to think about.

Zolotow pointed to a slippery clay ravine cut into the side of the bank, clotted with brush and a quarter sheet of corrugated aluminum stripped from some farmer's barn. "There," he said, "I'll hide there." He took his crutch back from her.

"And me," she asked, "where do you want me?"

He tried to smile. "Right there, darling. Just stand in the middle of the creek and look appetizing."

"I was afraid you were going to say that."

He probed the ravine with his crutch first, making sure there weren't any snakes. Then he wedged himself in, smearing himself (and the writhing snake) with red mud, dragging brush and the aluminum sheet over himself. "How do I look?" he asked. He had to repeat himself twice to be heard over the downpour and the thunder.

"Like an old bone Razor buried somewhere," she said. Then, "Quiet. Someone's coming."

They got lucky. The hunters could have divided their number based upon the directions taken by the three women. That would have left Zolotow with two men to ambush in this first encounter. Instead, two of the hunters had followed the false trail that Kendra and he had left, reasoning perhaps that they needed to take care of Zolotow first. It seemed to Zolotow like a strategy Caliber might have promoted.

The Right Reverend Willy Willis rounded a bend and splashed through the creek water toward Kendra, a beatific smile on his face, his arms outstretched, hands turned palm up and empty. Zolotow noted that the creek had risen several inches since they'd first come upon it. The prairie wasn't good at holding its water. He was reminded of the flash flood warnings broadcast on the afternoon news. Willis was wearing a yellow rain slicker, the hood down to reveal his wet, thinning hair and scrawny neck. His slacks clung darkly to his thin legs.

"Don't run, child," Willis said just loud enough to be heard over the rain. "You're safe. Let me help make you right with God. Let me show you his light."

Kendra raised her fists. "You keep coming, Preacher Man, and somebody's gonna see lights all right."

Willis didn't hesitate. "Tis a far better place you'll be going to. The Bible says that the meek shall inherit the Earth. Until that day comes, you'll sit with the children of God, at his feet, surrounded by beauty and light and unparalleled love." He reached out to her. "Take my hand. Let me show you the way home. Let me show you everlasting life in Heaven."

"You sick son of a bitch. What would you know about Heaven? You're too busy trying to buy your immortality here. The only everlasting life you'll ever know will be spent sucking Satan's backside."

"You're wrong, child. What I do, I do for the good of all mankind. The longer my time on this Earth, the more souls I can bring to the glory of God. I —" He heard Zolotow as the detective scrambled out of the ravine and splashed into the water. The preacher spun around and went into something that was meant to be a fighting stance. Kendra delivered a sharp kick to his calf, dropping him to his knees in the water. She drew back a hand to chop him across the back of the neck, but Zolotow was there by then.

Zolotow grabbed the Reverend's collar, raincoat and all, and ripped it open. "Let me be the first to introduce you to the serpent, Reverend Willis." He stuffed the rattler down Willis' shirt front and let go, snatching back his hand before the surprised snake could strike.

Willis screamed, falling in the water and thrashing about. Zolotow smacked him over the head with the crutch. "Shut up!" he yelled, thinking as he did it that Oklahoma must be rubbing off on him. He was using the local greeting now. Willis struggled away through the water, swatting and grabbing at his clothing which looked to have taken on a life of its own. If the raincoat hadn't been zipped up, he might have torn the buttons from his shirt and let the snake free. In his panic, however, Willis couldn't find the zipper. His weak attempts to rip open the slicker only jostled the enraged snake and inspired it to strike all the more.

"He'll bring the others," Kendra said as Willis went flopping and braying around a bend and out of sight.

"Couldn't be helped," Zolotow replied with a shrug of his muddy shoulders. "One down. Two to go." He took her hand in his. "Let's go."

The two remaining hunters overtook Zolotow and Kendra before they managed to catch up with Penny and Taneesha.

Zolotow turned in the creek bed, the water well above his knees now, to watch Caliber and Watson approach. The Governor was wrapped in the same sort of yellow slicker that Willis had worn, with the hood up, revealing nothing but shadow where his face should have been. Evidently, Brett Caliber had declined rain gear in favor of *machismo*. The actor's dress shirt clung to his pecs and biceps. When Caliber saw Zolotow, he grinned and ripped off the shirt. His broad, hairless chest was a golden brown in the next lightning flash. The tattered shirt spun away in the current, pale blue against the muddy red, briefly tangling with Zolotow's crutch.

Zolotow gave Kendra a gentle push. "Make a run for it."

Kendra held her ground at his side, saying nothing. Her eyes were as dark as the snake's had been.

"Take the bitch," Caliber told Watson. "The big guy's mine." He said more, but the rest of it was lost in a flash of lightning and a crash of thunder. The ground shook. The creek surged against Zolotow's thighs. The wind and the rain whipped about them.

  With the heel of his shoe, Zolotow popped the rubber cap off the tip of his crutch. He braced himself as Caliber rushed forward through the rain. Though probably just as capable as Willis at delivering speeches — How else had he become Governor? — Watson chose to attack Kendra in silence, lunging in Caliber's frothy wake. Kendra drew her butter knife and waited, her face set in what Zolotow would describe as resignation. She'd wanted an easier escape than this. And Zolotow suspected she knew that catching a drunk by surprise and kicking the shit out of him was different than the life and death struggle about to ensue. He wished he'd had more time to boost her confidence, to prepare her for this, but he'd done all he could in the time that he'd had. He noted, however, that she was smart enough to keep the blade concealed against her thigh until Watson was within reach. Her street savvy might save her yet.

  Brett Caliber stopped just out of reach of the crutch and did some flexing. "I'm going to take you apart, man." His fists were big. His eyes were bright and expectant. Before he'd become a half-ass actor, this man had obviously been in some brawls. The fact that he was still fair to look at did not bode well for Zolotow.

  Zolotow feinted high with the crutch. When the actor raised his arms, Zolotow reversed the weapon and tried to drive the sharpened tip into Caliber's thigh. But the creek bottom had sucked up around Zolotow's shoes, and he lost his balance. Caliber moved quickly, allowing the sharpened tip to slip off the side of his leg, ripping his expensive slacks, but doing little, if any, damage to his leg. Off balance, Zolotow stumbled forward. Caliber caught the crutch in his left hand and jerked Zolotow into a haymaker of a right. Zolotow saw lights, then the red water rising to meet him. He went under for a couple seconds. He expected Caliber to follow him down, to press him beneath the muddy water and hold him there, but Caliber danced back through the water, moving on his feet like Mohammed Ali on a tidal flat.

  Regaining the surface, Zolotow risked a glance at Kendra and Watson. Kendra had backed the Governor out of the water, nearly to the steep northern side of the gully, slashing at him with the butter knife. Watson's slicker was shredded in several places across the front and the arms, but he appeared uninjured. There was no blood. The governor was biding his time, dodging the majority of her thrusts. He didn't look concerned.

Caliber lunged in and put a front snap kick into the center of Zolotow's chest. Zolotow went over backwards, pain erupting from his solar plexus, the wind driven from him. He realized then that Caliber had studied karate at one point in time, might have even earned a belt or two. As the muddy red water closed over Zolotow's head again, he realized he was in serious trouble. Scrambling back, trying to regain his feet in the slippery mud, he lost the crutch. When he came up out of the water, gasping for air, Caliber was there, all slippery wet muscle and grins in the rain and the lightning. The actor delivered a quick combination of punches, most of which Zolotow managed to block, but a heavy jab slipped through and caught Zolotow on the chin. His legs went rubbery. Water closed over his head again. He came up choking, having taken in a lung full of water and liquid prairie.

"I really thought you were going to be more of a challenge than this," Caliber said, shuffling back through the water. Whether it was chivalry or just the fact that he wanted to prolong the fight, he was at least allowing Zolotow the opportunity to get to his feet after each exchange.

"Me, too," Zolotow gasped. He hated that he sounded so apologetic.

He risked another glance at Kendra and Watson. Somehow she'd made the mistake of coming to grips with the man. As Zolotow watched, the knife was taken from her hand. It vanished in the mud, having never really played a significant part in the struggle. All she'd managed to do was ruin a nice rain coat. Watson was obviously stronger than he looked. He lifted her and slammed her against the side of the gully. Pressing her head back into the mud, he bared her supple, brown neck.

Screaming, Kendra raised a knee that caught the governor in the groin. As the man stumbled back, she knocked his arms from throat. "Get off me, you son of a bitch!" She chopped him across the collarbone, followed up with a kick to the shin. "You're invading my personal space, you bloodsucker!" Watson stumbled back. She followed, raining blows on him. He'd either recovered from the low blow or most of it had caught him on the thigh, though, as he appeared to be blocking most of her fist work. A second later, he slapped her hands away and caught her with a punch that flattened her into the mud.

And then Zolotow had to attend to his own beating.

Caliber caught Zolotow with a series of punches that drove him back through the water. A roundhouse kick — something that Zolotow would have been embarrassed to have missed blocking on a normal day — caught the detective in the side of the head. He would have gone down, but the wind had suddenly come up behind him with gale force. Howling, it swept through the gully, bringing with it an even greater onslaught of rain. Zolotow wondered if he wasn't about to witness one of Oklahoma's famous twisters.

Blinking in the deluge, struggling against the wind, Caliber pursued Zolotow toward the southern bank of the creek. "Pay attention!" he yelled over the booming of the thunder when he saw Zolotow trying to check on Kendra. "At least *try* to give me my money's worth."

Zolotow opened his mouth to explain that he'd be happy to refund the price of Caliber's ticket, but another of the actor's punches slipped through and cut him off. He fell back, but managed to catch a glimpse of Kendra through Caliber's legs. Watson had her down against the bank. He had her by the hair and was slamming her head into the mud. Kendra was struggling, but weakly. She didn't appear to have much fight left in her.

Caliber grabbed Zolotow by the lab coat and pulled him back to his feet. "For a big guy, you're…"

Zolotow didn't give him time to finish. He'd heard that line once already, anyway. He hooked his bad leg behind the actor and shoved forward with his good one. Caliber went down into the water with Zolotow on top. Zolotow got in several quick punches. Though they connected, they did little damage as most of their energy was absorbed by the creek. It was enough to get him free of the actor for a second though. He used this time to lunge away, making for where Watson was beating Kendra senseless. He'd only gone three or four steps, however, when something locked tight around the ankle of his bad leg and jerked it out from under him. Once again, he went under the water, face first this time. Pain lanced up through his bad knee. His scream was only audible under water.

This time Caliber was mad, and he was tired of fighting by gentlemen's rules. He scrambled on Zolotow's back and pummeled the back of his head, holding him beneath the water. Again, the creek absorbed most of the blows. Zolotow dug down in the mud at the bottom of the creek and leveraged himself over. Upper body strength and the depth of the water paid off; there was no way Caliber could stay on him. Zolotow came up with great handfuls of prairie goo and slapped them into Caliber's face. The actor floundered back through the water, flailing at the mud in his eyes. Zolotow turned to go to Kendra's aid, but discovered that she was already getting help.

Taneesha and Penny had come back. The three women had Watson down against the bank, raining punches and kicks down on him. Three against one. The odds had definitely shifted on the good Governor. Reelection was looking unlikely. A pencil flashed in a strobe of lightning, slick with blood. Something else, glass perhaps, caught the lightning and threw it back.

Zolotow turned his attention back to Caliber. He was reaching for the garrote tied around his waist when the actor dove in low like a Dallas Cowboys lineman making a quarterback sack. Zolotow was folded over the man's shoulder, the air driven from his lungs again. Gasping, he tried to stay on his feet. Something clipped the side of his head. A fist — it must have been a fist. A rising knee caught him in the injured ribs. Another fist exploded against his nose. (Or maybe it was his nose that exploded?) Stumbling, Zolotow tried to stay vertical and keep his hands up. A fist caught him in the ribs again, the same ribs that had been introduced to Earl's baseball bat ... What, a day ago? It seemed like years. It seemed he'd been hurting forever. Another fist caught him in the face.

There came a sudden roar that was entirely separate from the drone of the rain and the pounding of the thunder. Zolotow thought the sound was in his head. *This is it*, he thought, *this is where I go down for good*. But the sound came from without, not within. He had just enough time to look upstream before a roiling wall of red water smacked him like a brick wall. Caliber yelled something. One of the women screamed.

The world turned upside down and inside out.

You hear about people getting caught in flash floods, and you think to yourself, well that's just plain ignorant. Water doesn't just go from ankle depth to over your head in a matter of seconds, does it? Surely, there's time to see it rising and get to higher ground. You don't just go lolly-gagging along some washed-out creek bed, waiting to see how high the water's going to get. Only an idiot would do that!

But like that guy scuba diving off the coast of California, sometimes you never know what's coming until it scoops you up and dumps your sorry ass in the frying pan. Sometimes you don't have time to worry about higher ground — especially when the ground on which you're getting your ass kicked is likely to be the last ground you'll ever see. Sometimes you just go with the flow because you're too fucked to fight back.

These were the thoughts that ran through Zolotow's mind as the mud and water ground him like a tablet in an apothecary's mortar. Tumbleweeds and submerged scrub brush tore at his face. Rocks pelted him. Whirlpools and eddies twisted his limbs. Something that might have been a hog's carcass all the way from Turpin, Oklahoma (but could just as easily, he thought in retrospect, have been the Right Reverend Willy Willis) slammed into his back and ground his face into the muddy bottom of the creek. He managed to fight his way to the surface, cough up creek bottom, and draw in what was mostly a mixture of muddy froth, before he was sucked under again. The creek took a sharp bend to the right, but failed to advertise the turn until the last minute. He was slammed against a sandstone wall which stripped the lab coat from his back, leaving him nothing but one tattered sleeve dangling from his right hand like a flag of surrender.

The second time he reached the surface, he cast about for something to cling to and came up empty-handed. Luck sucked him back under just as the creek took another sharp turn. He felt this one coming in the undertow. With all his might, he kicked up from the creek bottom to smack face first into the rocky bank. Flailing about like a madman, he managed to get his arms up above the flow of the water. With one Herculean heave, he pulled a waterlogged pulp of rags and lacerated flesh out of the current and into the mud. Only later, when he had managed to hack the mud and water up out of his lungs, would he fully realize that this battered golem was the Martin Zolotow he knew and loved.

For several minutes, he lay there and gasped, while the rain pelted his face and lightning left scars across his retina. He might have stayed there longer, but then he heard a gasping choke several feet away. He rolled over. The next flash of lightning revealed Brett Caliber not more than fifteen feet away, half in, half out of the flooded creek. It would only be a matter of minutes before the actor regained both his feet and his desire to see Zolotow dead.

Zolotow staggered to his feet and shambled away from the creek. He wasn't sure what had become of the ladies. If nothing else, however, he could lead Caliber away from them. If the women stayed with the creek — assuming, of course, that they hadn't been drowned by the flash flood — the creek might conceivably carry them far enough away to make an escape.

His crutch was lost, and it was difficult walking. The knee was singing in agony, but it was a song that he was, frightening and surprising as it seemed, learning the words to. Like Disney's "Small World," he was becoming inured to its litany. The leg folded under him several times, but he was moving better than he'd have expected in the soft mud. He didn't have to go far, though. Fifty yards into the blinding rain, he came across a house trailer. The broken windows and vacant, doorless entry told him that it was long abandoned, occupying land, perhaps, that McDevitt had bought up years ago. You don't want close neighbors when you're training your friends to be vampires.

There was a stock tank in front of the trailer, kept company by the skeletal frames of several lawn chairs, long since pillaged of their webbing by the panhandle's incessant winds. Seeing the chairs and a pallet which had been set on blocks to make a crude deck, Zolotow realized he'd stumbled across some redneck version of a swimming pool. If there was any doubt, there was a deflated toy — it might have once been a turtle — hanging over the side of the tank, long since bleached of color by the Oklahoma Sun. A trailer home and a galvanized steel stock tank for a swimming pool — what more could a man want out of life? "Cindy Lou, put on yer two piece and fetch my cooler of Bud. We're goin' swimmin'!"

The tank was filled to the rim with dark water. The carcasses of several unidentifiable rodents were bobbing lifelessly. A family of gophers, perhaps, having tunneled up through the rusted bottom of the tank, thinking they had found the ideal home, protected from the wind, only to be caught in this most uncommon rain storm. A couple squirrels that had fallen in and been unable to climb out maybe. Regardless, they were wet, indistinct lumps of fur now, bobbing about like Halloween apples. A plan came to Zolotow suddenly, a gift from that dark corner of his mind where such things were hatched and traded for random chunks of his memory. Despite the bobbing furballs, he didn't hesitate to put the plan into action. Ripping the sleeve from his arm, he tucked it into one corner of the pallet, where the sodden rag flapped weakly in the stout wind. He untied the knot on the garrote around his waist and wrapped the ends of the cord firmly around each of his hands. Then he slipped over the rim of the stock tank and sank into the fetid water within.

The water smelled of roadkill and motor oil. Its surface was a slimy sheen which might have yielded a lovely rainbow effect in sunlight, but beneath the thundering black sky it spoke only of putrescence and blood. It had a texture to it, like a thick, gummy gumbo. Zolotow sank to his nose and drew the deflated turtle about his head.

He waited.

"Zolo!"

Kendra. He recognized her voice.

"Zolo, where are you? Help me! It's Taneesha! Oh, God, she's not breathing!"

At that moment, he decided that the Fates had turned on him yet again. He was about to abandon his trap when Brett Caliber shambled out of the rain, following the deep, water-filled tracks Zolotow had left in the mud. Caliber spotted the tattered sleeve of the lab coat and made a beeline for it. Oh, what a tracker that boy was! Tonto would have been proud. As the actor bent to pull the rag free, Zolotow surged up from the black water, caught Caliber by the ears, and brought his forehead down on the rim of the tank. Before Caliber could react to that skull-splitting blow, Zolotow looped the lamp cord about his neck, twisted it over once, and drug the squealing son of a bitch over the rim of the tank and into the water, where he sat on his back and pulled the cord so tight that his shoulder muscles felt as if they would rip free of their ligaments.

Caliber squirmed and spewed a ton of black bubbles. Zolotow pulled against the garrote and howled at the lightning split sky, cords of muscle and tendon standing out on his neck and shoulders. "Now the hungry lion roars," he quoted from Shakespeare, "and the wolf behowls the moon!" Submerged in the foul stew of the tank, Caliber heard none of this. He squirmed and he fought, arms flailing and legs kicking desperately. He heaved and he twisted until his lungs forced him to suck in great gulping mouthfuls of black water. Zolotow felt those gulps as Caliber's ribs convulsed against the inside of his thighs. He didn't turn lose until long after Caliber quit moving. When the actor bobbed to the surface, his face all bloated and purple, his tongue protruding from his black lips, he looked like fitting company for the gophers.

"I never liked your fucking movies anyway," Zolotow told him.

"Zolo!"

He flopped over the side of tank, sprawling in the mud, scrambling back toward the creek. He found the women by following Kendra's voice. They were all three there, near a narrow stretch of creek where the flood waters had washed over onto the prairie flats. Had Zolotow hung with the flow a little longer, he would have probably emerged at the same spot.

Penny lay to one side, curled as if in pain. She was clutching her arm, which appeared to be broken. Kendra was bent over Taneesha, alternating between CPR and calling for help. It was obvious that Kendra had been at it for some time. She looked exhausted. Zolotow pushed her aside and took over.

"Come on, Taneesha," he panted while doing compressions on her chest. "Don't do this to me, darling."

"I drug her from the water," Kendra moaned, as if that had some bearing. And, a moment later: "The Governor of Oklahoma is dead."

"Ain't that a fucking shame," Zolotow panted.

Penny merely rocked and held her arm without making a sound. Her face was pale. Zolotow wondered if she was in shock, but he would have to deal with it later.

Zolotow breathed for Taneesha. Mother of two. Breathe. Master of the butterfly bandage. Breathe. Bathtub companion beyond compare. Breathe. As he started again on compressions, he saw her in her teddy pajamas, bent over the bathtub, soap suds running down her arms, slipping across her mahogany thighs.

"Come on, Taneesha," he begged.

Kendra stroked her face. "Please, Taneesha. Your boys need you."

The rain slowed down and, as if on cue, something howled in the darkness.

"What was that?" Kendra asked.

Zolotow ignored her, back to breathing for the beautiful dead woman laid out in the mud before him.

"Someone's coming."

Compressions. "Whoever it is, he'll have to wait his goddamn turn."

"Oh, God," she moaned, "it's Willy Willis."

Breathing. Zolotow glanced up on an inhalation. Willis had lost both rain slicker and shirt. His chest and stomach were mottled with angry purple welts, each trailing twin streamers of dark blood. There must have been two dozen of these swollen lumps circling his body. His hands and forearms were misshapen, swollen with snake venom. He was a shambling, zombie-like apparition, coming as he did out of the dark and the rain, his eyes all vapid, his swollen hands waving blindly out in front.

"Ahhhhhhh —" Willis wailed like something from a bad horror flick.

Compressions. Breathing. Compressions. Zolotow drew back his fist and let her have it right between the breasts. "Damn it, Taneesha, don't do this to me!"

The dead woman choked. Black bile and creek water gurgled in the back of her throat. He rolled her to the side and let her spit it all up. "Oh, fuck, that hurts," she cried. "Am I dead? A body ought not to hurt so bad if it's dead."

"Ahhhhhhh —" Willis wailed, as if disagreeing with her.

"You're not dead, sweetheart," Kendra said. Zolotow released Taneesha into Kendra's waiting arms, and drew himself up to deal with Reverend Willis.

Headlights pierced the night. Willis screamed and covered his eyes with a mottled purple and yellow forearm. Zolotow turned, twisting his knee so that he dropped into the mud. A Jeep emerged from the gloom. Billy Ray stepped out into the mud, rain sluicing from his cowboy hat. Bubba Uzi, whose brother Ernie had met with the misfortune of traveling with Earl, got out of the other side of the Jeep. Both men were armed with handguns, which they'd already drawn. A second Jeep pulled up beside the first and puked out two black men with shotguns. Tobias Weatherford Washington heaved his gargantuan body out of the back seat and stared with some distaste at the mud. Finally, he stepped down from the Jeep's running board, his fine lizard skin boots sinking nearly a foot in the mud. Though the rain was rapidly backing down, he raised an umbrella over his head.

"Who is it?" Kendra asked.

"Well, it ain't the fucking cavalry," Zolotow replied, "that's for damn sure."

Bubba pointed at Willis. "What the fuck is that?"

Billy Ray raised his gun and put a nice round hole in the Reverend's forehead. Willis fell like a dead tree, making a nice splash in the mud. "Don't much matter who or what it is now." Billy Ray pointed the gun at Zolotow. "You sit still, dickhead, or I'll send you right along after Mister Night of the Living Dead there."

"We need medical attention," Zolotow said.

"Shut up!"

Zolotow would have been disappointed if he hadn't said that.

Toby Washington, rain running from his oversized black umbrella, splashed through the mud to stand in front of Zolotow. The big mobster was breathing heavy. Walking in all that mud must not be easy for a man who can barely lift his feet off the ground.

"You're not looking so good, Zolo."

"Better than your man Ernie looks, though." Zolotow pointed to Billy Ray. "You'd better ask that son of a bitch what kind of deal he and Earl cut with McDevitt."

Billy Ray stepped around Washington and shoved the muzzle of his revolver against Zolotow's forehead. "I told you to shut up!"

Zolotow ignored him. "Earl and Billy Ray sold you out, Washington. First they worked me over with a baseball bat to make sure I couldn't bring your daughter back. Then, I saw Earl open Ernie up with a 12 gauge. This morning they fed what was left of poor old Ernie to the hogs."

Bubba stepped forward, his mouth open and his eyes wide. "Ernie's dead?" he asked in disbelief.

Billy Ray cocked his .357. "That's it for you, Zolo."

Washington drew his own gun, a snub-nosed little Ruger .38. "Hold on, Billy Ray."

"You haven't heard from Earl since you sent him out here, have you?" Zolotow asked. "You sent him to collect your daughter after you gave me and Coop up to McDevitt, but Earl and Ernie never came back, did they?"

Washington made some sort of little hand signal. The two men with shotguns stepped up behind Billy Ray, their guns trained on him.

"I saw Earl murder Ernie," Zolotow repeated. "Then, just this afternoon, Earl was sitting in one of Jimmy McDevitt's lawn chairs, sipping beer, whittling, and whistling a country western tune. 'My Heroes Have Always Been Cowboys,' I think it was."

"You're a lying sack of shit," hissed Billy Ray.

Washington pointed his Ruger at Billy Ray. "Back off. I want to hear what the private eye has to say."

The muscles along Billy Ray's jaw clenched. His nostrils flared. His eyes were mean little slits. "He's lying, Toby. Let me open him up right here in the mud. We don't need him anymore."

"I said back off, Billy Ray!"

Billy Ray stepped back, but he didn't lower the hammer on his .357.

To all their surprise, Penny suddenly got to her feet. She was trembling and ghostly pale. She held her twisted arm close to her side. She was chewing her lower lip in pain, but her eyes were clear and her head was up. "Zolo's telling the truth. Billy Ray's working for Jimmy McDevitt. I saw him there."

Billy Ray switched his aim to Penny. "Shut up, whore!"

"Jimmy lets the boys take turns with us. Billy Ray's come to my bed more than once. Earl, too."

Billy Ray looked to Washington. "She's lying, Toby. They made this shit up to try and distract us. They're wanting us to fight amongst ourselves."

Washington rubbed his .38 against the wattles on his neck, thinking. Finally, he looked to Penny. "You got any proof, woman?"

Penny just stared. "Proof?"

"Yeah. How the hell do I know you didn't make this up? If you're lying to me, I'll kill you right here and now; so you'd better come clean."

Penny looked as if she was going to sit back down. Then, quite suddenly, she smiled. "I got proof." She nodded toward

Billy Ray. "That cowboy's equipment is crooked."

"How's that?"

"His pecker," she explained. "It bends to the right."

"What?"

"You heard her," Zolotow chimed in. "Man's got a crooked dick."

"This is ridiculous," snorted Billy Ray. "I've never seen this bitch before in my life."

Washington turned back to Billy Ray. "You want to drop your trousers and prove she's lying?"

"What? You want me to show you my dick?"

"It ain't crooked is it?"

"Well, hell, no, my dick ain't crooked!"

"Then drop your drawers and show me."

"Fuck that!"

Washington pointed his gun at Billy Ray again. The other three men did the same. To Zolotow, the two shotguns, in particular, looked to be worth displaying one's personnel equipment.

Billy Ray looked desperate.

"Crookedest damn dick I ever saw," Penny chuckled.

"I think I might have seen it, too," Kendra added. "Sumbitch could fuck around a corner."

"Toby," pleaded Billy Ray, "I've been working with you for years now. You gonna believe me or a couple whores?"

Washington's face softened. "Look, Billy Ray. All you got to do is show me your equipment. We'll clear this whole matter right up."

Thunder rumbled off across the prairie, sounding distant and weak. The rain was now just an annoying drizzle. The moon tried to peek out from behind the clouds.

Billy Ray swallowed. He nodded his head and reached for his silver belt buckle. Then he shot Toby Washington.

All hell broke loose. Washington shot back. The two shotguns roared as one, loud as the thunder just ten minutes ago. Bubba emptied all six rounds from his revolver and turned as if he was going back to the Jeep for his Uzi. Billy Ray just kind of disintegrated where he stood, frozen for a second in a haze of vaporized blood. The shotguns roared again and Billy Ray went down to his knees and hovered there, blood cascading down his hips and thighs from a midsection that was mostly gone, courtesy of the shotguns. Washington stepped forward and shot him twice in the head sending his cowboy hat spinning away. Billy Ray fell over in the mud.

Zolotow wiped Billy Ray's blood from his face.

Kendra screamed, "Penny!"

Penny was down, the right side of her sweater red with blood. One of the shotgun blasts had caught her beneath the arm and in the breast. Zolotow scrambled over to her and ripped her shirt open to assess the damage. She was losing blood, fast. Zolotow applied pressure best he could. He needed a compress, but his shirt was gone. More importantly, he needed to get help for her fast. "I need to get this woman to a hospital," he told Washington, *"now."*

Washington tossed down his umbrella and probed his side. His hand came away covered with his own blood.

"You hurt, boss?" asked Bubba.

"Nah," Washington replied, "it's just a fat wound. Ha! Get it? Like a flesh wound!" He showed Bubba where Billy Ray's bullet had passed cleanly through his side.

"This woman needs an ambulance!" Zolotow shouted at them.

Washington frowned, pursed his fat lips.

The crack of a high powered rifle suddenly rolled across the prairie. One of the two men with the shotguns dropped his weapon and went down like a stone.

"Shit!"

Washington and his men scrambled for cover behind the Jeeps.

"Move!" Zolotow yelled at Kendra and Taneesha. "Behind the Jeeps, quick!" Zolotow lifted Penny in his arms and, running on adrenaline that dulled his many aches and pains, he ran with her to the Jeep. A rifle barked again. Something angry whined past his ear. Then he was behind the nearest Jeep with Toby Washington, Bubba, and the girls. The other man with the shotgun scrambled behind the second Jeep. A bullet shattered the Jeep's windshield and screamed off into the night.

As Zolotow reapplied pressure to Penny's severed arteries, Washington pulled a cell phone out of his pocket. "You'd better be dialing nine one one," Zolotow growled.

Washington pointed his snub nose at the detective. "Sit tight, Zolo." Bubba had reloaded. He pressed his gun against Zolotow's back.

Washington speed dialed. Someone quickly answered at the other end. "Yeah, it's me, Toby Washington. Listen up, asshole. I done found some interesting shit out here on the prairie. I got a famous actor floating belly up in a stock tank. I got some preacher I saw on the TV once leaking his brains out into the mud. And word is, the Governor of Oklahoma is on his way to the Gulf of Mexico. Ain't that some wild shit for a night out on the prairie?"

The rifle boomed again, followed closely by a second shot which had to come from the other rifleman. The Jeep shuddered with the blows.

"Yeah? Well, I think you know a lot more about the shit that's going on out here than you're letting on, Jimmy. I also got some women and a real pain in the ass California private eye here. I think they know more about what's going on than you'd care to have show up in the *Beaver Chronicle* or, God forbid, the *USA Today*. 20/20 might even want to have them on. If nothing else, I'm thinking they'd have a lot to tell the State Police or the FBI. So, you don't call off them boys with the rifles right now, I'm going to give this private eye the key to my Jeep, Jimmy. I'm betting he makes it outta here. I'm betting he squeals like a motherfucker when he does. What do you say?"

Several moments of silence.

"I need an ambulance for this woman," Zolotow pleaded. "God damn it, she's bleeding to death!"

Kendra squeezed his arm. "Zolo…"

"Shut up," Bubba told them.

"Good. Now here's what I propose. I want my daughter, Jimmy. That's all I want. I want my baby. What? Hell, no, I don't already have her! Who? My daughter's name is Rayleen.

Rayleen Washington. I never heard of anyone named Kendra. I don't care what the hell some whore told you. My daughter's not here. You find her. You hear me? You find her right now!"

"Get him to send an ambulance!"

"Zolo…"

"I'll trade you Zolotow and these whores for my daughter. Ten minutes, Jimmy. In ten minutes I'm driving up into your front yard. I see one man with a gun and I'm turning around and heading straight for the feds. You understand? You send my daughter out, and I'll give you Zolotow and his whores. Don't you double cross me, you son of a bitch. Don't you dare double cross me!"

Washington switched off the phone and slipped it back in his pocket.

Zolotow reached out with a hand drenched in Penny's blood and made a grab for the phone. "Damn it, man, you can't just let her bleed to death!"

Weeping, Kendra tried to pull him back. "Zolo, she's gone."

"No," Zolotow moaned.

"She's gone, Zolo. She's gone."

"Noooooo!" Zolotow howled at the black sky. "Damn you! Every fucking one of you!" he screamed. "I'll kill every fucking one of you before I'm done! I swear to God I will!"

Bubba cracked him over the skull with the butt of his pistol. Zolotow dropped lifeless into the mud. The moon broke free of the clouds and looked down on the flooded prairie with indifference.

Interlude: "Let's talk anger, let's talk violence –"

"— let's talk body counts."

"Why is it," Zolotow retorted, "no one ever wants to talk *results*?"

"Oh, I'm not questioning your results, Detective." She tapped the stack of paper on her desk with a meticulously manicured, red nail. "Yours is the most impressive record I've ever seen. There's no doubt about that. I'm questioning your procedures. I'm questioning the long line of dead men behind you."

He faked outrage. "This department has sent me after the vilest of criminals over the years. I've been assigned to take down the absolute dregs of humanity, the lowest vermin on this planet, and then you wonder that they resist arrest? You wonder why I've put so many of them in the ground over the years?"

Ellis put on her clinical psychologist face. He had all her faces memorized by now, had labeled each and every one and knew most of the verbiage that followed them. "I'd like to know, Detective Zolotow, who you're still trying to save out there?"

He wondered then if maybe his file was more complete than he thought. He wondered if she knew about his mother. He wondered if she also knew the truth about his father. Was he still trying to save his mother after all these years? Did he regret not putting a bullet in his father's skull?

He said something then that he shouldn't have, something he knew he'd regret later, but it came out before he'd thought it through. Once said, there was no way he could take it back. It would go down in his records. It would haunt him every time he shot another bad guy. Every time Internal Affairs ran him through the grilling that he already knew by heart.

"Sometimes I ask myself," he said, "why we bother to arrest them at all. Most of the ones we arrest wind up back out on the street committing other crimes. I think we'd be better off just shooting them the first time."

She actually smiled, though he couldn't tell if she was amused or if she felt as if she'd just won something. "Are you familiar with Nietzsche's writing, Detective? Have you read what he had to say about those who fight monsters being careful that they don't become monsters themselves?"

"'And if you gaze for long into an abyss,'" Zolotow quoted, "'the abyss gazes also into you.' I know it."

"And...?"

He smiled right back at her. "Lady, I live in that abyss. I call it home. When the abyss gazes into me, it trembles."

Six: *The Cavalry (at last) and Man's Best Friend — Whup Ass and Coat Racks — Pig Shit and Oklahoma Drivers — Wheelchairs and Country Music Appreciation*

Penny's long, luxurious hair tickled his face as she bent to kiss him. "It's okay, Zolo." Her lips were warm and soft against his forehead. He was wet and cold ... shivering uncontrollably. Some joker had replaced his testicles with ice cubes. "You did everything you could. Nobody can say you didn't try." She kissed him again, warming his frozen lips.

"I'm sorry," he whispered, his voice weak and distant, as if lost in a dense fog.

"Shush," she said. "You rest now, honey. You're only human. Only one man. No way you could save us all. You're nobody's white knight, darling." She set her hand against his face.

"That's what Debbie said."

Somewhere in the fog, a car door slammed.

"As soon as they trade us for her, we're dead."

"Debbie?"

"Rayleen, you idiot." She slapped him.

He could hear distant voices ... two men talking. Despite the fog, their Midwestern drawls came though loud and clear, even if what they were saying did not.

"Rayleen's not even old enough to drive yet," he mumbled, realizing even as he said it that it made absolutely no sense at all.

She slapped him again. "Wake up, Zolo!"

He opened his eyes and Penny's face underwent one of those computer morphing effects, rearranging itself until he was staring up at Kendra, her face all creamy chocolate in the moonlight, except for swollen bruises beneath one eye and above her lip. They were in the back of one of the Jeeps. Zolotow was laid out across the seat, his knees tucked up to his chest, his head on Kendra's lap. He was soaked through and through. His hands were encrusted with Penny's blood. There was more of her blood on his arms and chest. Kendra's shirt was stained with it.

Kendra drew her hand back to slap him again. Weakly, he reached up and caught her wrist.

"Where?" he mumbled through swollen lips. He hurt all over. He couldn't remember a time when he hadn't been hurting. The same joker that had messed with his testicles had left a butane torch going in one of his ears.

"Jimmy's front yard," Kendra said. "Washington and one of his goons are walking to the front porch right now to talk to Jimmy. Taneesha's in the back of the other Jeep. Washington's other goon, the one with the shotgun, is keeping an eye on us."

"I don't suppose they left the keys in the ignition?"

She frowned and looked like she wanted to slap him again.

"What happened?"

"You freaked when Penny got shot, started screaming about how they were all dead men. One of them knocked you over the head. Then they tossed us in the Jeep ... but they left poor Penny out there in the mud." Her voice caught, and she had to fight back tears. "That was only about fifteen minutes ago."

"Oh." Most of it came back to him. "God, I'm cold."

"I know. Fucking Washington ran the air conditioner full blast all the way here. Fat people sweat like pigs."

"Help me sit up."

"They're gonna trade us for Rayleen, and then we're dead, Zolo."

"I heard you the first time. Help me sit up." What was coming back stronger than anything else was his anger. It swelled from deep within him, a fire that fed off his pain, that swallowed the butane torch in his head, that boiled in his blood and screamed in his mind. This was why he was no longer a cop. He hadn't the faintest interest in seeing these people arrested. He wanted them dead. And he wanted to be the one who sent them to Hell.

When he was sitting up, he took stock of their situation. The spotlights on the front of the house were all lit up, just like the night he and Johnson had tried to make their getaway. Had that really been just last night? The helicopter and the limos were gone. McDevitt's Mercedes and a couple pickup trucks were there, though, parked closer to the house. Washington had left his vehicles near the main road, as if he thought that gave him some assurance that McDevitt wouldn't attempt to screw him on the trade. Washington and Bubba were crossing the big yard, almost to the front porch now. McDevitt was waiting, along with Coop in his wheelchair and two other guys; one of them might have been Digger, but it was hard to tell in the shadows that cloaked the porch. It was easy to spot McDevitt, though, big and pale with the moonlight shining off his bald dome and those broad shoulders bulging out of his coveralls. There was no sign of Earl. Maybe McDevitt thought it best if Earl stayed out of sight. No one on the porch had a gun in sight. Zolotow vaguely remembered Washington making it clear that the deal was off if he saw firearms. Washington and Bubba were keeping their own handguns under their jackets. Zolotow wondered about the two men with the high powered rifles. They could be almost anywhere. The black man with the shotgun was standing between the two Jeeps, his weapon held at port arms.

The smell of pigs was back, full strength. The stench only made him madder.

Zolotow pointed to the man with the shotgun. "Roll down the window," he told Kendra. "Call him over here."

"What do I do when he gets here?"

"Distract him."

"How?"

"Think of something. Quick. My brain's not working too good yet." Actually it was working fine, but the capacity for clever subterfuge had been sacrificed to the fire coursing his veins.

Kendra pulled the snake's rattle out of her shirt pocket. "Penny was hanging on to this like she thought it might come in handy. I took it before they threw us in the Jeep."

"That'll work. Call him over. And, Kendra? When the shit starts flying, get the hell out of here. This is it. One way or another, the games stop now." That said, Zolotow slumped against the seat and tried to look as if he was still unconscious.

Kendra rolled down the window, which immediately

got their guard's attention. He pointed the shotgun at her. "Roll that window back up!"

"Help," she said, doing an incredible job of looking terrified. Zolotow watched her through slitted eyes, thinking there might be a career in acting for her. "I think there's a snake in the Jeep!"

"A snake? How the fuck's a snake gonna get in there with ya'll?"

"Please, you've got to let me out of here! It sounds like a rattlesnake!"

"Ain't no fucking rattlesnake that could climb up in a Jeep, lady." The man stepped closer, but he was still covering her with the shotgun. "I think you done lost your mind."

"No, please. Listen, if you don't believe me. Come closer to the window and you can hear it. I think it's under the seat."

Frowning, he lowered his gun and stepped up to the window. "You try anything, bitch, and I swear I'll hit you so fucking hard your mama'll cry." As he leaned in the window, Kendra shook the snake's rattle, which she was holding out of sight under her leg. The black man's eyebrows went up. "Holy shit! That do sound like a rattler!"

Zolotow grabbed the man by the neck and hauled him as far in through the window as his shoulders would allow. Dropping down between the seats, Zolotow twisted, using his body weight, leveraging the man against the door. Kendra tried to reach past him and get her hands on the shotgun, but the window was blocked by his shoulders.

It's not as easy to break a man's neck as Hollywood would have you believe. The vertebrae and connecting ligaments actually have a lot of play in them. Zolotow had done it once before in his life, but he'd had his full strength then. What he lacked now in strength, he made up for in sheer anger and adrenaline. The bastards had killed Penny. They'd killed Daryl Johnson. They'd threatened, and possibly even killed, Debbie. They'd hunted innocent young women and fed who knows how many other victims to their hogs. He'd taken all he was going to take from them.

The sound a neck makes when it finally lets go is something you can feel. Its crisp pop! echoes in your gut, twisting coldly from your scrotum up to the base of your skull. You feel it in your bones as if your own neck's been broken. It's a sound you never forget.

When the black man's neck snapped, he let out a squall like a newborn infant. Zolotow let him go, and the man hung there in the Jeep's window, the only muscles in his body still receiving signals being those in his face, which had contorted into something ghoulish. Hollywood would have you believe a man with a broken neck simply drops dead without a sound. Sometimes that's the case. Other times, the poor bastard's eyes dart left and right in absolute terror and he screams his lungs out, knowing good and well what's been done to him.

Kendra stared at the screaming man hanging on the door. She'd gone pale. She looked like she was going to be sick. "You broke his fucking neck," she muttered in disbelief.

Washington and Bubba were just starting up the steps to the porch when they heard the screaming. They turned, saw the guy hanging out the window of the Jeep, and started running back across the yard, drawing their handguns.

"You broke his —" She couldn't bring herself to say it again.

Zolotow reached across Kendra, turned the door handle and shouldered it open. "Say a prayer for him later," he hissed at her. She flinched from what she saw in his eyes.

As the door swung open, dragging with it the man with the broken neck, Washington and Bubba started shooting. One bullet shattered the windshield. Another thunked metallically into the door. Zolotow scrambled over Kendra and grabbed the shotgun from the ground. Tumbling from the vehicle, he pushed off the safety with his thumb. A bullet slapped wetly into the injured man's chest. The next one took off the tip of his chin, thrust up toward the sky where he hung over the door. Zolotow rose from behind the man and opened up with the shotgun. At this distance, the pattern was spread pretty wide. Bubba caught the first blast and did a little dance, cursing. He and Washington both fired again. Both shots hit the guy hanging on the door. Mercifully, the guy went silent, his terrified eyes rolling back into his head.

Zolotow worked the slide on the shotgun, expelling a smoking, red plastic shell. He took aim on Bubba again and fired. The big black man stumbled and went down to one knee. Washington hesitated, looking at his henchman, wondering if it was wise to rush Zolotow while he had the shotgun. Zolotow pumped another shell into the chamber, stepped out from behind the door, and shambled across the yard, firing. One, two, three, and the shotgun was empty. Bubba was down, though, his face gone. Washington was stumbling back toward the house, his fat torso slick with blood.

McDevitt and his people had retreated into the house, going for cover or their own weapons.

Though he fell several times, Zolotow overtook Washington. He reversed the shotgun in his hands, holding it by the hot barrel, and brought it down over Washington's skull. The shotgun's stock split from butt cap to breach. Washington went down to his knees, his rolls of bleeding fat bouncing obscenely. He tried to turn and bring his little .38 to bear, but Zolotow knocked the gun from his hand with the shotgun. Washington looked up, his beady little black pig eyes bright with fear. Zolotow raised the shotgun again, ready to cave in his skull.

"Freeze! Federal Marshals! Drop the gun!"

Zolotow turned to discover two dark sedans had pulled up behind the Jeeps. Kendra and Taneesha were running toward them, being waved on by someone in a Navy blue suit and a red tie just visible over the top of his bullet-proof vest. There were six Marshals in all, crouched behind their cars with shotguns and M-16s. Headlights in the distance revealed two more vehicles enroute.

The cavalry at last!

"Drop the gun!" The man doing the shouting had stepped out from behind his car and was crossing the yard, his automatic rifle trained on Zolotow. Obviously, they didn't know how to tell the good guys from the bad guys.

Zolotow let the shotgun slip through his fingers. It splashed into the mud. He was opening his mouth to warn the Marshal about the men in the house, when he caught movement from the corner of his eye. Someone rose to his feet out by the pig pens. The barrel of a rifle was leveled over a hog trough. Moonlight reflected off a scope. The gun barked and the Marshal's throat exploded, spraying blood down over his bullet-proof vest. From over near the building where the women were housed, another rifle boomed. The agent standing and waving the women to safety suddenly grabbed at his chest and went down. It was impossible to say whether he was wearing a vest under his clothing because he was wearing a light weight jacket zipped to his throat; regardless, he didn't get back up.

The breaking of glass preceded more gunfire from the house. The men behind the sedans returned fire and suddenly Zolotow was caught in a crossfire. He was about to dive to the ground when Washington surged to his feet and caught him up in a massive, bloody bear hug. Blood streaming from where Zolotow had opened up his head with the shotgun, Washington bellowed like a mad bull and squeezed. Veins stood out on either side of Washington's neck. His bloodshot eyes bugged out of his skull. Zolotow howled in pain. The two men shuffled back and forth in the mud, bullets zipping past their insane little dance. The only reason they weren't hit was that, for the moment, the shooters were intent on eliminating each other.

And then Kendra was there. She kicked Washington several times in the kidneys. When this had no effect, she retrieved his .38 and shot him in the back. Washington faltered and the crushing grip on Zolotow lessened slightly, but he did not go down. Kendra pulled the trigger again, but there was nothing but a dry, sharp click as the hammer dropped on an expended round.

"Get him off me," Zolotow groaned.

Kendra picked up the shotgun and struck Washington over the head again. A piece of the cracked stock flew away, bouncing off the porch steps. When she drew the shotgun back for another blow, Washington howled and dropped Zolotow into the mud. He turned, knocked the gun from Kendra's hands, and backhanded her across the face. Kendra went down. Zolotow tried to get up, but he couldn't seem to refill his lungs. His ribs didn't want to expand to their accustomed position. Washington reached down and caught Kendra by the hair. He was dragging her to her feet when a dark shape shot out from under the front porch, growling like a chainsaw at full throttle.

The rottweiler caught the big man by the throat and hung there, growling and shaking its head back and forth, working its jaws through the thick layers of fat and cartilage surrounding Washington's windpipe. Washington tried to pull the dog off, but Razor hung on. Blood gushed out over the dog's black lips and darkened its muzzle. Zolotow, some of his wind back, kicked out, taking Washington off his feet. Washington hit the mud with a great splash, the dog still tearing at his throat. Washington's fat legs kicked at the sky (a stray bullet snapped off one of his heels in a moonlit spray of red) and his fists pounded at the dog. Razor refused to let go.

"Good boy, Razor," said Kendra.

"Rip his fucking head off," added Zolotow. The dog merely cocked its eyes at Zolotow and growled as if to say the detective might be next, then he went back to chewing at Washington's throat. The sound of crunching cartilage and the snarling dog was an eerie accompaniment to the rattle of gunfire.

Four of the six Marshals were down (though one was crawling weakly toward a radio microphone dangling from the open door of his car). Their vehicles were riddled with bullet holes. Taneesha was under one of the cars, her arms over her head, trembling. There was no way to ascertain if there were any fatalities in the house, though bullets had taken out all the front windows and pock-marked the siding. The two riflemen were untouched, casually taking aim on visible limbs, pinning down the two remaining federal agents, one of which had already been shot in the leg. Over the sharp reports of the rifles rattled the staccato of automatic weapons from the windows of the house. The other two sets of headlights seemed to have disappeared, awaiting instructions perhaps, or maybe they were circling around to the back.

A sloppy operation, thought Zolotow, but maybe they hadn't anticipated much resistance from a hog farmer in the Oklahoma panhandle. Perhaps the initial six Marshals had planned to wait for those in the other vehicles to take up positions, but Zolotow had jumped the gun and fouled their plans by launching his own assault.

One thing was obvious: he couldn't wait for them to save the day.

Zolotow grabbed Kendra's arm and scrambled with her toward the porch. "Under there!" he yelled, shoving her toward Razor's hideout.

"What about you?"

"Vengeance is mine," he said, hurling himself up the porch steps.

The front door was a solid oak affair, thick and heavy, but he gave it his all, launching his full weight against it. He was beyond feeling pain. It was the frame that gave way, splintering from the studs of the house so that the whole assembly, door and all, came crashing down in the tiled foyer of the house. Zolotow went rolling across the floor, taking out a brass coat rack and a small phone table. There was a formal dining room to the left, a closet on the right, some sort of parlor or sitting room straight ahead. From the dining room, Digger turned away from a window, aimed a nine millimeter, and opened fire. Zolotow rolled past the dining room doorway as several bullets skipped off the tiles and splintered the fallen door. Another slug tore through the wall, splattering Zolotow with powdered gypsum. By this time, he'd snatched up the coatrack and was rushing the sitting room dead ahead.

Behind him, Digger burst into the foyer, intent on shooting Zolotow in the back. Kendra stepped through the gaping doorway behind him. Hearing her, he spun around. She kicked the pistol from Digger's hand, chopped him across the neck with a right, put her left fist in his eye, and then spun on the ball of one foot, her other foot sweeping up and around to connect with the side of his head. A classic, beautifully executed spinning hook kick. Her brothers would have been proud. Digger slammed into the wall, leaving a football-shaped dent where his head hit the wall paper.

"Second time I kicked your sorry ass!" Kendra told him.

A hail of bullets peppered the front of the house. Kendra dived into the dining room, but Digger was left standing there, reeling from Kendra's kick. Four M-16 rounds stitched a tight little line up the side of his face, opening up the entire back of his skull as they expanded and made their exit. All six foot four of Digger went down without a sound.

Zolotow caught all of this out of the corner of his eye as he surveyed the parlor. To one side there was a hallway from which he guessed bedrooms opened off, situated across the front and west sides of the house. From several of these rooms, he could hear gunfire. Several bullets had passed through the rooms and left holes in the far wall of the hall. To his right there was a stairway leading up to the second floor. Just around the stairway landing was a wide doorway which opened on what appeared to be a living room. Beyond the living room, he could see a kitchen. Standing in the middle of the living room, arms folded casually over a shotgun, was Jimmy McDevitt.

Zolotow brandished the coat rack over his head and charged, screaming a battle cry that would have made

Alexander the Great tremble.

Earl was standing just to the side of the doorway, out of sight. As Zolotow rushed by, the redneck clipped him with a fist to the back of the head. Zolotow went down, the coat rack clattering across the hardwood floor. Had the punch hit him solid, Zolotow would have probably been finished. As it was, his head was reeling when he rolled over to discover who had clubbed him.

"I can see it's way past time for opening another can of whup ass on you, boy," drawled Earl, his voice barely audible over the clatter of the gunfire from the front of the house.

Zolotow shook the stars from his eyes. He tried to reach the coat rack, but Earl picked it up and stood it to one side, next to a television that had succumbed to a stray bullet. Earl removed his hat and hung it over a hook on the rack. He ran his fingers back through his greasy hair. His blue eyes sparkled. "Yessir, one can of whup ass, coming right up."

"I hope you brought a really big can," Zolotow croaked.

"Big enough," Earl chuckled. "You go on ahead," he said to McDevitt. "Get what you need from the lab, and I'll meet you out back by the hogs." He cracked his knuckles. "This won't take long."

McDevitt hesitated. "I don't know, Earl. I'd kinda like some time with Zolo myself."

Earl shook his head. "Sorry, boss. You know what needs salvaged from the lab. I don't. Those feds have probably already called for backup. We ain't got much time. I'll meet you at the truck out back of the hog pens."

McDevitt gestured with the shotgun. "Then we just blow his damn head off and be done with it."

"Hell, where's the fun in that? I tell you what, this sumbitch has got worse coming to him."

Zolotow pushed himself to his knees. "Where's your baseball bat, Earl? You don't look nearly so tough without it."

"We'll see about that," said Earl. He put the toe of one of his cowboy boots into Zolotow's ribs. Zolotow went back down to the floor with a grunt.

"Shit. You girls have your fun, then." McDevitt slung the shotgun over his shoulder. "Don't expect me to wait around long for either one of you, though." Then he turned and ran out through the kitchen.

"I'll try not to be long, Jimbo," Zolotow called after him, but he didn't think the big, bald man heard him.

Earl reached down and caught Zolotow by the hair and pulled him up off the floor. "May I have this dance?"

"No," replied Kendra, suddenly stepping up behind him. "I'm cutting in." She kicked Earl in the back of the head.

Earl stumbled, but did not go down. This wasn't Digger, who'd spent most of his time drinking in the kitchen. Earl turned and blocked a combination of punches that Kendra threw. Then he threw one of his own and Kendra toppled back into the couch where she lay on soft gold pillows, looking as if she'd suddenly decided a nap might be nice. There was blood running heavily from her nose. Earl turned back to Zolotow, a wicked grin on his face.

But Zolotow was up and waiting.

He brought the coat rack down over Earl's head. Earl stumbled back, raising his arms to defend himself. Zolotow brought the base of the coat rack around and cracked it against the side of Earl's knee. "How's that knee, Earl? Hurt? Pity I don't have a baseball bat!" He brought the coat rack up and then down again, breaking through Earl's defense and splitting open his forehead. "What's that? I can't hear you, Earl?" The coat rack made a pleasant bell tone as it rang off Earl's forearms and head. *Bong!* "Say something clever, you stupid redneck son of a bitch!" *Bong!*

Earl curled up on the floor. Zolotow pounded his ribs and back, struck him a couple more times across the knees. By the time Zolotow realized Earl was covering up so he could pull his nine millimeter from a shoulder holster, it was almost too late. But he spotted the gun in time, mainly because Earl was one of those morons who thought a nickel-plated gun was cool. In the dim light of the living room, Zolotow might have missed the weapon had it not been such an eyesore. Zolotow broke Earl's elbow with the coat rack. The gun spun away across the hardwood floor which, by this time, was speckled with blood. More of Earl's bright red body fluid was running down the length of the brass rod, pooling against the webbing between Zolotow's thumb and forefinger, running across the back of his knuckles and down his forearms, where it mingled with Penny's dried blood. Gulping air, Zolotow spent another minute pounding Earl with the coat rack. When he finally had to quit before he collapsed from exhaustion, Earl was a blubbering, bleeding mess on the floor.

"I quit," Earl moaned wetly. "I don't wanna play no more."

Zolotow dropped the coat rack and collected the pistol from the floor. He stopped to check on Kendra. She was out cold, her nose still bleeding. It was probably broken. A career in modeling might be out of the question. Tenderly, Zolotow swung her legs up on the sofa and made her comfortable. The rottweiler came through the door, its muzzle and chest slick with Washington's blood. Zolotow pointed to Earl, curled in a red fetal ball on the floor. "You're too late, pup. I had to take up the slack for you." Razor growled at him and took up a position near Kendra.

"Don't let that fucking dog near me," Earl whined.

Zolotow checked the pistol. There were six rounds left in the magazine, one in the chamber.

"Go ahead and arrest me," Earl said, spitting up blood. "I'll go quietly. I have the right to remain silent..." He tried to laugh, but a vicious cough cut it short.

"I know all your rights," Zolotow said softly, working the pistol's safety with the side of his thumb. "You have the right to remain so fucking silent, they'll swear you were dead." He raised the gun and put one of the seven remaining bullets through Earl's brain. Earl's head thumped wetly to the floor and he made not a sound. He just lay there leaking on the nice oak floorboards, a pattern of blood, brains, and bone chips spread on the floor behind him.

Razor walked over and sniffed at the dead man once, then looked at Zolotow with something like approval — and, maybe, just maybe, a new-found respect. *Of course*, Zolotow decided, *I might just be imagining it.* When he reached out as if to touch the dog, Razor growled and snapped at his hand.

"Fine. You just stay here and watch Kendra, mutt."

The rottweiler's response was to bury his face in her crotch and sniff happily. Zolotow went through the kitchen and out the back door toward the lab, following McDevitt.

Zolotow fell twice crossing the back yard to the lab. Had he not fallen, he might have missed the parallel ruts leading through the mud from the back door of the house to the lab. Either the rednecks had taken to riding bicycles back and forth between the two buildings... or Coop had gone this way.

He put two bullets into the lock mechanism, then hit the metal door with his shoulder. It held. He shot the lock again, mentally ticking off the remaining rounds in Earl's nickel-plated S&W as the expelled brass bounced off the side of the building. Something metallic came loose and fell with the door. Hearing this minute sound, only then did he realize that the gunfire from out front had stopped. The moon was still riding high in the sky. The clouds had moved off to the east where distant lightning still kissed the plains. Visibility was good. Zolotow could see the rifleman out by the hog pens, scanning the front of the house through his scope. The man by the women's building was either gone or better concealed. Since neither was shooting, the agents out front must all be dead.

Grunting, Zolotow shouldered the door again and it gave, hanging on by just a last few screws. Remembering that McDevitt was armed, Zolotow stepped to the side of the door and thrust it open. The roar of a shotgun shattered the sudden stillness. Pellets scored the aluminum door frame. Knowing how long it took to work the pump gun, Zolotow ducked low and leaned into the opening, squeezing off two of his three remaining rounds.

McDevitt was halfway across the room, standing beside an Einstein-clone wearing a white lab coat. Both men clutched an armload of file folders. McDevitt also had a large plastic box of floppy diskettes under his arm. One of Zolotow's shots punched through a stack of files and caught McDevitt in the upper arm; the other spun around the guy in white. The spinning man screamed, his clown hair making his pirouette almost comical. Paper went flying. The diskette box dropped, shattered, and diskettes scattered across the floor. McDevitt fired again, but his aim was high, thrown off balance by the bullet he'd taken in the arm. The door's lintel exploded, raining metal fragments down on Zolotow's head. Rolling, Zolotow advanced through the doorway. Another shotgun blast went over his head and burst a 50 gallon plastic drum, spilling an amber fluid out over the floor. Choking on the fumes from the spilled chemical, Zolotow came up behind a desk. He sighted quickly around a computer monitor and fired his last round.

McDevitt, however, had caught the Einstein look-alike and yanked him around as a shield. As Zolotow's bullet caught the guy just below the collarbone, Zolotow spotted the name stitched above his breast pocket. Einstein was, in fact, the mysterious Dr. Alahandro. As Alahandro fell, McDevitt opted to let the doctor drop so he could make a run for the storeroom exit. Going through the door, McDevitt turned and fired again, blowing the desktop monitor to pieces. Interrupted electricity crackled. Sparks flew. *Whoomf!* The amber fluid went up like a pool of gasoline.

Zolotow rolled across the top of the desk, flames licking at his bare back. The nine millimeter, its slide locked open to indicate it was empty, went clattering across the floor. As Zolotow ran past, Alahandro caught his ankle and nearly brought him down. "Help me!" screamed the doctor. The shoulder and the side of his lab coat were red with blood. His eyes were wild. Zolotow kicked free of his weak grasp and rushed through the burning room to the storeroom door. In every film he'd ever seen, the mad scientist went up in flames with his installation. Who was Zolotow to change that?

McDevitt was waiting in the storeroom, near the back door, shotgun aimed. Zolotow ducked to the ground outside the doorway. A shotgun blast opened a head-sized hole in the wall above him. The plate from a light switch ricocheted off the top of his head. Zolotow stayed low, waiting. Flames were sweeping rapidly across the room, climbing the insulation along the walls, spreading across the ceiling. Beakers and canisters of volatile fluids were exploding. Computers and other sensitive equipment popped, showering sparks, components, and glass. Fluorescent bulbs exploded, raining glass down from the ceiling. The lights flickered and went out. Obviously, McDevitt had not invested in a sprinkler system. The room was quickly engulfed.

Alahandro began to scream with more than terror. The burning fluid continued to pour out over the floor at a speed which exceeded the rate at which it was burning. There were other plastic drums in the room. As the fire spread around these drums, they melted, spewing more fuel for the fire. Crawling in his own blood, the doctor attempted to get clear, but the fluid overtook his legs. His clothing caught fire. His skin quickly followed. The smell of roasting flesh mingled with the smoke and chemical fumes.

Over the roar of the fire and the screaming, it was impossible to hear the back door slam. Zolotow had no idea if McDevitt was waiting for him, but he couldn't wait any longer. Flames were licking at his feet and dripping from the ceiling around him. He was choking on the smoke. He waited a full minute, then cautiously ducked his head around the base of the door. The storeroom was empty. The floor here, like the floor in the lab, was marked with the muddy tracks of a wheelchair and McDevitt's boots.

Zolotow scrambled through the doorway and hobbled across the smoke-filled room. Behind him, something exploded in the lab and flames leapfrogged out into the storeroom. He cracked the back door and peeked out. McDevitt was nearly to the hog pens. There, the rifleman was down, clutching a chest wound, and a Federal Marshall was standing over him, kicking the rifle out of the prone man's reach. Evidently, the second group of vehicles had circled around the back. As Zolotow ran from the burning lab, McDevitt raised his shotgun and shot the Marshall. The Marshall was wearing a vest, but the force of the 12 gauge took him off his feet. Cursing, he went down in the knee deep pig shit and mud. McDevitt stopped at the fence and took aim on the squirming man's head. He was about to pull the trigger when Zolotow tackled him from behind. The two big men hit the wooden fence. The dry, old panhandle-weathered railings snapped. Both men fell through and into the pig pen.

As he tried to get to his feet in the thick sludge, Zolotow heard pigs squealing in the shadows near the hog sheds. All the gunfire would have terrorized them. Now there were a couple madmen destroying their home. McDevitt was the first one up. He cast about for the shotgun that he'd dropped, but it was lost in the wallow. Zolotow came up behind him and leaped on the man's back. He knew he hadn't the strength to wrestle the man, but he feared even more standing toe to toe with him. McDevitt reached over his shoulder, wrapping his arms around Zolotow's neck. If he'd had the full use of both his arms, he might have been able to bring Zolotow over his shoulder and hurl him to the ground again, much as he'd done the night Daryl Johnson was murdered. As it was, the best he could do was swing Zolotow around to the front, where he drew back his fist and threw a punch that would have shattered Zolotow's jaw had it connected.

Zolotow leaned back just out of reach of the punch. Flecks of mud and pig shit flew from McDevitt's fist and splattered his face. Squealing, something squirmed out from under Zolotow's feet. As he fell, he saw a dozen piglets trying to make their escape. Before he could even hit the mud, four hundred pounds of sow charged up through his legs. For a split second, he was riding the hog, then he slipped off its backside as it bowled right over McDevitt.

The sow and the piglets went stampeding across the yard, squealing as if wolves were hot on their heels. Had Razor been outside, the dog could have had a field day chasing them.

Both men scrambled to their feet at the same time. McDevitt's cheek bore the angry red imprint of a pig's foot. The hog farmer caught Zolotow by the throat with both hands, intent on crushing his windpipe, but Zolotow sank his thumb into the bleeding bullet hole in McDevitt's biceps. McDevitt howled. He hurled Zolotow back into a solid post. Stunned, Zolotow sank down the length of the post, coming up short when his ass plopped into the mud.

The agent who'd shot the rifleman was back on his feet, searching the pig pen for his pistol. McDevitt rushed him and clubbed him over the head with his doubled-up fists, driving the agent face first into the muck, where he lay without moving. McDevitt turned back to where Zolotow was trying to catch his breath against the side of the post.

"Now to snap your fucking neck," McDevitt gasped, "then make my getaway." There was pig shit running down his chin and stuck to the side of his head. It looked like he was hoarding a gallon or two of the stuff down the front of his coveralls. Firelight gleamed off the exposed portions of his bald plate. His sharpened canines were incredibly white bright triangles of ivory in the moonlight. His pale blue eyes were glassy and hard, like marbles.

Zolotow nodded toward the burning lab. "Make your getaway —" He was still gasping for breath. "— without your life's work, though, asshole. You and your vampire club are out of business."

Around the corner of the house came three more Federal Marshals.

Seeing the agents, McDevitt abandoned Zolotow. He tried to leap the back fence of the pen, where presumably his getaway truck was waiting just behind the hog sheds, but his mud-clogged boots caught on the top rail. He went sprawling on the other side.

"It's over," Zolotow yelled as the big man scrambled to his feet.

McDevitt's face suddenly lit up, like a cartoon character with a light bulb going off over his head. He reached into his filth-covered overalls and withdrew his Beretta, looking as if he just remembered that he was carrying the damn thing. "I'll see you in hell," he told Zolotow. He took aim.

Zolotow didn't have time to tell him that he was probably right about that statement.

A bright red 4x4 pickup truck careened around the corner of the nearest shed, all four tires slipping and sliding in the mud, engine roaring at full throttle. It slammed into McDevitt. He went down beneath the front tires, which chewed on him a second and then spit him up under the truck where he bounced once or twice off the undercarriage. One of the rear tires crushed Jimmy McDevitt's head like a watermelon and churned him out the back end. He rolled up in the mud, twisted and bleeding, brains mixed with pig shit and prairie, which, thought Zolotow, was somehow ironically appropriate. As the truck accelerated north out into the prairie, Zolotow caught the slogan on its mud flaps.

If you ain't country, you ain't shit.

He saw one other thing before the truck was lost in the darkness. In the rearview mirror, from which hung an IV bottle, he'd seen a pale, maniacal face lit by the light of the burning lab. Ice colored eyes magnified all out of proportion by thick glasses. Cheeks so red they looked like they were bleeding. Hair like porcupine quills. And a middle finger raised defiantly.

"God damn Oklahoma drivers," Zolotow chuckled. Laughter hurt. Breathing hurt. Being alive hurt. He closed his eyes and focused on the post against his back and the soft ground under his ass. He worked on his breathing and tried not to notice the stench. He concentrated on staying conscious and waiting for help.

"Amigo?" Someone shook his shoulder. "Talk to me, you smelly son of a bitch!"

Zolotow opened his eyes and grinned. "What took you so fucking long?"

Hector Garza returned the smile. "So, you're not going to die after all, eh?"

"I'll live to see you shoveled under, you overweight beaner."

"Hey! At least I don't send important email to Hernando Garza out in Seguin. You try sending your email to the right place, *pendejo*, and someone might be able to come rescue your sorry ass a little quicker!"

"Oh, no. Debbie? What about Debbie?"

Garza squeezed his shoulder. "The *senorita* is fine, my friend. We picked up Herman Munch —"

"Herman Munch?"

"Bruiser. You called him Bruiser in your email. He wouldn't talk, but we checked his phone records and traced a call made from a cell phone registered to someone named James McDevitt. When we confronted Munch with the phone records and explained to him about being an accessory, he told us plenty about McDevitt."

Zolotow nodded toward the mess lying in the tracks left by the truck. "Meet Jimmy McDevitt."

"I'll cuff him in a minute," Garza snickered.

"Go easy on him," Zolotow said. "He's not feeling so hot."

"Oh? And you are?"

They both laughed.

"Kendra?" Zolotow asked.

"That's the *senorita bonita* I found sleeping on the sofa?"

"Yeah, you can't miss her. She's got a dog the size of a horse keeping an eye on her."

"*Si*, that's the one. That damn dog tried to bite me! She's fine, Zolo. Paramedics are looking at her now. She'll be out as soon as they say she's okay."

"Don't let anything happen to her. She means a lot to me."

Garza rolled his eyes as if to say, *don't they all*.

"There are some other women in —"

"We're taking care of it, Zolo." Garza gave his friend's shoulder another squeeze. "Rest easy now."

"How about getting me out of this pig shit?"

"I don't know," said Garza. "Perhaps I should not move you."

"Screw that!"

"All right. You do smell worse than a Tijuana outhouse." He grabbed Zolotow under the arms and hauled him up. "Come on, *amigo*. I found a wheel chair behind these sheds."

"Cooper's chair."

"The guy in the truck?"

"Yeah."

"Feds are trying to get a chopper up now. They're a little slow, but this Cooper won't get far."

They heard a ringing coming from McDevitt. "What's that?"

"I don't know," Garza replied. "It sounds like a telephone." He leaned Zolotow against the post and walked over to McDevitt's corpse. "It's coming from this poor bastard." He poked around a bit, a grimace on his face. "Something tells me this old boy isn't going to be doing too well with the ladies, Zolo." He found the phone. "*Hola? Si.*" He shrugged and handed the phone to Zolo. "It's for you."

When Zolotow put the phone to his ear, the first thing he heard was country music.

> *He was born ... in Oklahoma,*
> *And his wife's name ... was Betty Lou Thelma Liz.*
> *He's not responsible for what he's doing*
> *Cause his mother made him what he is.*

"Zolo, you sorry sack of shit," squawked the phone, "you still alive?"

"Barely."

"I tell you what, it's a damn shame old Jimmy don't know to look both ways 'fore crossing the street, ain't it?"

"Jimmy never struck me as being the real intelligent type."

"No sir. He wasn't. He surely wasn't. But he'd a damn sure killed your sorry ass if I hadn't a crunched him under my pick 'em up truck. You owe me, boy. Know what I mean?"

"I hear you."

"So I'll see you later, hoss?"

"Not if I see you first."

Coop chuckled. "See if you can't go on and learn to appreciate a little of God's music in the meantime. Okay?"

> *And it's up against the wall, redneck mother,*
> *Mother who has raised a son so well.*
> *He's thirty-four and drinking in a honky-tonk.*
> *Just kicking hippies' asses and raising hell.*

The line went dead. Zolotow tossed the phone into the pig shit. "Let him go, Hector."

"What?"

"I said let him go. He saved my life. He's dying anyway."

"You sure about that?"

Not really, Zolotow thought. Maybe they *had* cracked the code there at the end. Maybe Coop would live forever. *If so*, Zolotow thought, looking at what was left of the lab and all the information that it contained going up in flames (not to mention Dr. Alahandro), *Coop would be the only one.* Well, maybe not. If one scientist had figured it out, it was only a matter of time before another one did. Soon you'd be buying it on the street.

Yeah ... right. When pigs fly...

Epilogue: *White Knights and Little Girls*

Garza pointed through the windshield as he shut off the engine. "That's the house."

"You sure?" Zolotow was doubtful. It looked too perfect. Too suburban middle class. He couldn't understand why she'd ever run away. He understood that sometimes things just don't go the way you plan them, though. Most of his life had been that way.

"*Si*, I am sure," Garza replied. He reached in the back seat and dug a beer out of a cooler. "I've never gone up and rang the doorbell or anything, but I saw them go in and out a couple times while I was trying to locate Munch and keeping an eye on her."

Zolotow checked his new watch. "You're sure she gets home about six-thirty?"

"Yeah, the library shuts down at six. It takes her about thirty minutes to get home."

Zolotow shifted in the seat of the cramped little rental car, trying to get at his hip pocket. Count on Garza to go cheap on him and rent a subcompact. His leg was hurting. The brace was wedged up against the dash and he couldn't straighten it out. The doctor had told him another three weeks and he could probably walk without the brace. Zolotow didn't tell him that he'd already been hobbling around the house without it for two weeks.

He pulled out the picture of Debbie sleeping in the hammock. Stained and creased, it had somehow survived the Oklahoma panhandle, much as he had, only slightly worse for wear. He set the picture on the dash where it caught the sun and, if he didn't study it too carefully, looked almost new.

"Kendra working out okay?"

"Yeah, except for that damn dog." Zolotow chuckled.

"Any time I want to be alone with Kendra, I toss a steak in the spare room. He goes in after the steak and I lock the door behind him."

"Must be true love, then. Steaks are mighty expensive."

"Must be. I tell you, Hector, that girl's got me thinking. Maybe it's time I tried to settle down."

"You and me both, *amigo*. There." He pointed again. "There she comes."

The Montgomery's mini van turned into the driveway and stopped. The driver's door opened. Debbie stepped out. She was wearing an ankle length skirt and a demure blue sweater. Sensible shoes. A book bag over her shoulder. Her head was up. Sunlight claimed her hair.

Garza reached for his door handle, but Zolotow put a hand on him and shook his head.

"You're not going to talk to her?" Garza asked.

"No, I just needed to see her. To make sure she was all right."

"Long way to come just for that."

Zolotow shrugged. "Appreciate you meeting me here."

"*De nada.*"

"She studies every night?"

"Damn near. College ain't easy, you know."

"No ... I don't."

No one had made sure that he went to college. No one had watched over him and made sure he didn't become just another of life's roadside fatalities. Foster homes had never agreed with him — his own fault, he wasn't fooling himself about that — and, despite years of looking, he'd never found his mother. As for his father ... well, he'd lied to Kendra that night. He had always known who his father was. His mother had told him.

Zolotow had finally tracked him down, during a long, hot summer vacation just before his promotion to detective. He'd found him in Bakersfield, barely surviving in a rundown trailer park, crack cocaine cooking on the stove, a young prostitute sleeping with him to feed her habit, letting him pimp for her whenever cash ran thin. Zolotow had held his service revolver against the bastard's head, had cocked it and tried to pull the trigger. Between alternately begging for his life and demanding to know who Zolotow was, Zolotow's father had wept. Zolotow never told him who he was. Nor did he pull the trigger. He'd simply turned and left him crying on the filthy floor of the trailer. He never saw him again.

He'd taken the young prostitute with him though. She'd turned out to be fourteen years old. In time, Zolotow had tracked down her parents and sent her home, where he presumed she was still living something close to a normal life. *We're all of us entitled to a normal life*, thought Zolotow. Family and friends. Safety. Comfort. A mini van and a hammock in the back yard.

The front door of the house closed behind Debbie and she was gone. He sat there feeling empty, feeling old.

"Kendra know where you're at?" Garza asked.

"Nah, she'd kick my ass," laughed Zolotow. He reached back, grabbed a beer, and popped the tab. "Come on, let's get out of here."

Garza started the car and pulled away from the curb. "You're not serious about retiring?"

Zolotow thought for a minute. Then: "Nah. I'd rather be a meteor."

"How's that?"

"Never mind." Zolotow smacked his can against Garza's, slopping foam in his friend's lap. "Here's to good friends and beautiful women."

> *I would rather be a superb meteor,*
> *every atom of me in magnificent glow,*
> *than a sleepy and permanent planet.*
> *The proper function of man is to live, not to exist.*
> *I shall not waste my days in trying to prolong them.*
> *I shall use my time.* — *Jack London*

ACKNOWLEDGEMENTS

Over the years, I've been asked not only the dreaded "Where do you get your ideas?" question more times than I can count, but also "Where do you get your story titles?" Believe it or not, there really is a Licking Valley Coon Hunters Club. I found it listed in the Yellow Pages while searching for a bar in a very dry county in Ohio. I didn't know it was a dry county; I only knew that I hadn't seen any clubs. So I went looking through the yellow pages. For some reason, I found it extremely hilarious to find a club based on the hunting of raccoons. Perhaps it's a pretty common social institution? I tore out that page of the phone book and saved it, determined that it would one day be a story title. Honest Injun. So, a thank you is owed to the real Licking Valley Coon Hunters Club in Newark, Ohio though they've no idea their bloodthirsty little sporting club inspired such a twisted tale.

The Licking Valley Coon Hunters Club was something of a writing experiment. You see, there were sixty some odd "voyeurs" in the writing of this story, some silent, some very vocal, all of whom have earned my gratitude. Though other authors have recently made some big (and bogus) claims to having been the first to ever serialize a novel as email installments, the fact remains that I did exactly that with *Coon Hunters* in the Summer of 1998. Not only did I serialize the novel, but I did it as the novel was being written. I'm just not arrogant enough to presume that I did it first. It seems such an obvious thing.

I admit to having been somewhat nervous when I started sending out installments of *Coon Hunters*. I mean, after all, I knew next to nothing about most of my audience. Had the story been written and polished beforehand, I would have been a lot more comfortable with the concept. It's not easy letting so many people in on the creation of something like this. There were an awful lot of opportunities for me to make a royal ass out of myself (and, perhaps, there were even a few incidences where I did so). Few writers, I think, will open their creative process to such scrutiny. The most valuable thing returned for the chance to watch me pen the tale was encouragement and support. Writing can be very frustrating. No writer does it for long without some serious bucks or some serious encouragement.

So, much appreciation is due all of the "Coon Hunters." There are some I need to mention by name — my pointing them out does not in any way diminish my sincere appreciation to the rest. In no particular order, thanks to: Sheila Wakely, Mike Marks, Jeff Vaughn, Rick McIver, Chris Anemone, Tim Lowrimore, Susan Burgard, Brett Savory, Judy Sadler, Debbie Hills, Karen Connell, Ken Abner, John DiPalermo, Barry Hunter, Mike Huyck, and Delice Weaver.

Many thanks to my good friend and frequent collaborator, David Niall Wilson, for not minding when I took what had been a shared character (Zolo first appeared in our two novellas, "*La Belle Dame Sans Merci*" and "*La Belle Dame Sans Regrets*") and went off on my own with him. Over the years, Dave has taught me much about writing and about myself. He's one in a million.

I am indebted to the following two sources of information concerning the genetics of aging: Michael Fossel (*Reversing Human Aging*, Morrow, 1996) and John J. Medina (*The Clock of Ages*, Cambridge University Press, 1996).

I am also indebted to both Joe Lansdale and Neal Barrett. It should be obvious that their work has had a great deal of influence on mine.

And, as always, I owe much to my family, Betty, Derek, and Summer. This book is for them, as well as the Scarecrow's Lady, the Poetess, and what dreams may come.

Martin Zolotow will return soon in *The Shady Grove Humane Society*. Promise. Feel free to bug the crap out of me about it at brian_a_hopkins@sff.net.

Brian A. Hopkins
at Road's End
Oklahoma City, OK
September 1999

Biography: Brian A. Hopkins

Brian A. Hopkins has published more than sixty stories in a variety of professional and semi-professional magazines and anthologies, including *Dragon Magazine*, *Aboriginal SF*, *Realms of Fantasy,* and the Stoker Award Winning anthology *Horrors! 365 Scary Stories*. 1995 saw the publication of *Something Haunts Us All*, a collection of Brian's short stories. In December of 1997, Brian's short novel, *Cold at Heart*, was published as a trade paperback. *Cold at Heart* received high praise and was nominated to both the preliminary ballot for HWA's coveted Bram Stoker Award and SFWA's Nebula Award. Known for his innovative use of email and the Internet to reach his readers, Brian released a 30 story anthology on a limited edition CD-ROM entitled *Flesh Wounds*. As Lone Wolf Publications, Brian is also producing a CD-ROM anthology, *Extremes: Fantasy and Horror from the Ends of the Earth*. Brian appreciates feedback and can be reached online at brian_a_hopkins@sff.net. He maintains an Internet home page at http://www.sff.net/people/brian_a_hopkins/.

About the Cover Artist

Brand Whitlock is an award winning artist who has done several covers for Yard Dog Press as well as the cover for Gary Jonas' The Curse of the Magazine Killers. Brand is currently working on interior art work for an upcoming Meisha Merlin Publication.

If you would like to know more about Brand and his work, visit our web site at http://www.yarddogpress.com.

Mark Tiedemann

Selina Rosen
#1 in
The Host Series

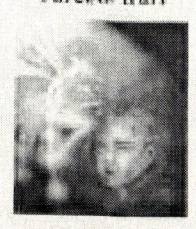

Edited by
Selina Rosen

Selina Rosen
#2 in
The Host Series

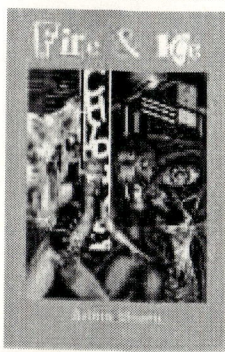

Selina Rosen

Selina Rosen
#3 in
The Host Series

Beverly Hale

James K. Burk

John Urbancik

Edited by
Selina Rosen

Jax Laffer

Lee Martindale

Mark Shepherd

Laura
Underwood

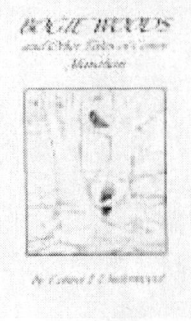

Bradley H.
Sinor

Stories from
Yard Dog
Comics

From the Yard Dog Comics

Gary Jonas

Bill Allen

Beverly Hale

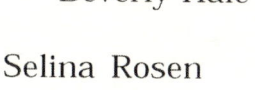

Selina Rosen

Selina Rosen
with collaborations from Bill Allen, Beverly Hale, and Brand Whitlock

Gary Moreau

An anthology of recollections of 9/11 compiled to help a Kansas City family that lost a loved one.

Three Ways to Order:

1. Write us a letter telling us what you want, then send it along with your check or money order (made payable to Yard Dog Press) to: Yard Dog Press, 710 W. Redbud Lane, Alma, AR 72921-7247

2. Contact us at srosen.lstran@juno.com to place your order. Then send your check or money order to the address above. *This has the advantage of allowing you to check on the availability of short-stock items such as T-shirts and back-issues of Yard Dog Comics.*

3. Contact us as in #2 above and pay with a credit card or by debit from your checking account. Just go to our website and sign up for PayPal. It's free, it's safe, it's easy. If you already have a PayPal account, it's even easier!

Watch our website at
www.yarddogpress.com
for news of upcoming projects and new titles!!